The Internet
KILLER

The Internet
KILLER

Daniel Warren Krygsveld

The Internet Killer
Copyright © 2020 by Daniel Warren Krygsveld. All rights reserved.

No part of this publication may be reproduced, stored in a retrieval system or transmitted in any way by any means, electronic, mechanical, photocopy, recording or otherwise without the prior permission of the author except as provided by USA copyright law.

The opinions expressed by the author are not necessarily those of URLink Print and Media.

1603 Capitol Ave., Suite 310 Cheyenne, Wyoming USA 82001
1-888-980-6523 | admin@urlinkpublishing.com

URLink Print and Media is committed to excellence in the publishing industry.

Book design copyright © 2020 by URLink Print and Media. All rights reserved.

Published in the United States of America

Library of Congress Control Number: 2020916448
ISBN 978-1-64753-468-4 (Paperback)
ISBN 978-1-64753-469-1 (Digital)

18.08.20

Contents

The Accident 7
Prison 21
A New Beginning 73
A Different Life 81

The Accident

At 18 Luke was looking forward to starting college in the fall, where he was enrolled in computer sciences. His parents were able to pay for his first year's tuition.

His agility, swiftness and 6 foot 4 stature had earned him a partial scholarship playing basketball in high school. This scholarship was enough to cover most of his books and computer equipment. He took a job at a local hotel as a valet to earn enough money for the other expenses that would crop up during the upcoming year. He still lived with his parents and the college was a short distance from his home.

He enjoyed parking the luxury and exotic cars the hotel patrons drove. One day a customer drove up in a BMW M5. Luke was very impressed with the car and commented on how luxurious it looked.

The Valet supervisor, John, a man in his late 30s, handed a receipt ticket to the owner of the BMW as he gave John the keys.

With a rye smile on his face, John looked at Luke, "Do you want to know what success feels like?"

Luke looked at him with a smile on his face. He knew John meant taking the BMW for a drive on the open road.

"No we can't do that", said Luke. "It's against company policy".

"Hey I'm the supervisor, if I say we can, we can."

John tossed a get in look at Luke and got into the passenger's seat, setting his cane beside him. John had severely injured his leg in a skiing accident years before and need a cane for added support.

Luke got into the black BMW and marvelled at the exquisite interior, tan coloured leather seats, wood grained steering wheel, and the smell of new and expensive. Luke started the engine and spent a few minutes adjusting the seat and mirrors and revelling in the sheer joy of the occasion.

With John buckled in, Luke started off slowly getting a feel for the car.

He turned onto the street beside the hotel and quickly accelerated to the posted speed limit.

"Let's go to Price Street and see what this machine can do." said John.

Luke quickly headed the car to the little-used street a few blocks away. Luke knew the street well. It was where he grew up and where his parents still lived.

Once there he looked down the street as far as he could see. No traffic, no pedestrians.

Luke gingerly pressed on the gas pedal, the car responded immediately and soon they were speeding down the road, gaining speed with each passing second. The BMW quickly reached 100 mph.

John was laughing and yelling "faster, faster".

Luke pressed harder on the gas pedal accelerating the car to 125 mph in seconds.

Price Street was divided in two parts. The first part was uphill and the second part was down hill. At the crest of the hill a driver could not see what was on the other side.

John, squirming and laughing with excitement, yelled faster ... faster. Luke eased up on the gas pedal. The BMW started to slow down. Luke knew the dangers present at the top of the hill. He had seen many speeding cars get air borne as they sped up the hill.

John looked at Luke, "What are you doing?" and at that John took his cane and pressed down hard on the gas pedal. The BMW lurched forward instantly hitting 150 mph. "No" Luke yelled, as he was about to dislodge the cane pressing his foot on the gas pedal.

But it was too late. The crest of the hill was in front of them. The BMW hit the crest of the hill and continue to climb momentarily. All four wheels were off the ground. Seconds later the nose of the BMW started to lower and the car still air borne was parallel with the road below.

John released his grip on the cane and grabbed the dashboard to brace himself. His face was white and a look of sheer terror distorted it.

Luke instinctively slammed his foot on the brake. Being still in the air the four wheels instantly stopped turning. Luke had a death grip on the steering wheel. His eyes closed.

Luke didn't see what was coming. His jaw set, his eyes closed, his arms out stretched from the steering wheel pushing himself back into the seat.

On the road just ahead of them a car, a Corolla, was pulling out of a driveway. The BMW impacted the Corolla just above the driver's door pushing the roof down and toward the passenger. The impact was so hard that the Corolla was crushed into the road causing the tires to flair out and the bottom of the car to scrape along the road. Inside the BMW the airbags deployed. The passenger airbag pushed John's arms up and back as it exploded from its casing. The force was so intense that the arms flew towards John's head and knocked him unconscious. Luke was hit in the chest and face with the airbag. His arms being on the lower part of the steering wheel were pushed down and back and ended momentarily pinned to his side.

Luke was still conscious and at this time opened his eyes to see the BMW flip end over end. The car impacted the road, 20 feet away from the Corolla, on its rear buckling the trunk. The car then tumbled forward and started to roll and finally came to a stop two blocks away against an aluminum light pole.

When the carnage was over, Luke was still in the driver's seat his hands had found the steering wheel again and he was clenching it for stability, the air bags in shreds around him.

Luke was still conscious but in shock. He didn't move, his legs were pinned down by the dashboard and his head was tilted sideways from the roof of the car pressing down.

Debris covered the two blocks that the car had travelled. The car that was hit by the BMW was unrecognizable. The two people in it were dead. John was dead. When he was knocked unconscious he flailed around with only the seat belt keeping him from flying out of the car. John had hit the passenger door several times and his cane had broken, with part of it sticking in his neck. Parts of both cars littered the road and neighbouring lawns.

When the rescue teams arrived it was just a matter of cleaning up the mess and putting people in body bags.

Luke had to be cut out of the BMW. Both of his legs were broken, his left arm was broken in two places and he had cuts to his face, arms and torso from flying glass and metal.

Luke was transported to the hospital where he laid unconscious for three days.

"Well, you're awake," said a soft young voice.

Luke focused his eyes on who was speaking. A young woman about his age, blonde hair, fair skinned, slender figure, about 5 feet 8 inches tall, stood at the foot of the bed.

She was giving him a sponge bath and was looking him straight in the eye. "I was wondering how long it would be before you woke up."

Luke turned his head to see where he was, then fell asleep again.

Several hours later he woke up again. This time he was a little more alert and realized he was in the hospital. He surveyed has body. His left arm was in a cast and his right arm was wrapped in bandages from his upper arm to his wrist, his legs had steel rods protruding from them with clamps and cross rods stabilizing his leg and ankles. He looked down to his chest and his mid-section was taped up.

Luke laid in the bed a tear coming to his eyes. He shook his head and tried to think of something else other then the condition he was in.

"Who was the woman I saw earlier," he thought to himself. "Was she real or did I dream of her?" He drifted off to sleep again and didn't wake up until the next morning when he heard someone come in the room and place something on the over-bed table beside him. He opened his eyes and saw someone leaving the room. On the table was a tray of food … breakfast.

He looked at his left arm that was in a cast and then at his right arm that was tapped up. Neither one would bend so that he could feed himself and surely unable to reach the table to bring it closer.

"Good morning, sunshine," said the sweet young voice again.

"Hi," said Luke. "You are real. I thought you were a dream."

"That's a first," she said. "I'm Nancy, a nurse's assistant."

"Hi Nancy," said Luke with a smile.

Luke looked at his arms, first at his left arm then turned his head to his right arm.

"You have a compound fracture in your left arm mid way between your wrists and elbow. You have a severe slash in your right arm which took 36 stitches to close. Both ankles are broken as well as the tibia just above the ankle and the femur just above the knee," she said softly.

Nancy raised the head of the bed to an upright position. "Is that comfortable there?" she said when Luke was in a sitting position.

"Yes, thanks," said Luke.

"Breakfast, I hope you like oatmeal?" said Nancy as she brought the over-bed table to the bed. On the table was a tray with a bowl of oatmeal, a glass of orange juice and fruit. "Bon Appetite," she said with a smile and standing back a step to see his reaction.

Luke looked at the food on the tray and again at his arms. Then he smiled and looked at Nancy, "nice, girl, bring it closer and I'll lap it up."

They both laughed and Nancy pulled up a bedside stool and started to feed him.

As Nancy feed Luke she talked about going to college and getting her nurses degree and become a full time paediatric nurse.

Luke expressed his desire to become a computer engineer. Which he had doubts about given his current situation?

That afternoon the police came in and formally charged Luke with auto theft, reckless driving and vehicle manslaughter in the death of three people. "An attorney has been appointed as your legal advisor and he will be in contact with you shortly", they said as they left.

Luke looked over at the paper that the police left on the table beside the bed.

"Nancy would you hold up those papers so that I can read them," he said, motioning to the papers on the table.

"Sure," said Nancy and she picked up the papers and sat on the bed so that she could hold the papers properly while he read.

Tears came to his eyes as he read the names of the victims of the car crash.... John Slather, Marie Dawson, Jim Dawson......

"What's wrong Luke," she said putting the paper down.

Luke looked at Nancy and motioned her to read the paper with the charged laid against him.

Nancy looked at the paper and immediately saw what upset him. "I'm so sorry Luke," she said stepping closer to the bed and putting her hand gently on his shoulder. "Marie and Jim are your Parents!" Tears came to her eyes also as she gave Luke a kiss on the forehead and left the room.

Luke's appointed lawyer arrived about a half hour after the police left.

"Luke, I'm your lawyer, David Ruth," he said as he pulled up a chair beside the bed. "A time has been set for your court case, which in your condition you won't be physically able to attend."

"We will set up a video link to the courtroom so that you can participate in the proceedings." "For now though I want you to tell me what happened leading up to the crash," said David.

Luke told David the story.

David sat quietly for a few minutes thinking. "I think we should put in a plea of not guilty and go with a …" David was saying.

Luke interrupted, "I'm going to plead guilty," he said.

"If we stated the circumstances of the reason for the joy ride we might turn the court in your favour."

"No," said Luke. "Guilty and make a deal with them that I can go to school and get my computer engineer degree."

"We have a good chance of winning this," said David.

"And if we don't what would the sentence be?" asked Luke.

"In past cases the sentence has been 10 to 15 years," said David.

"If I plead guilty, what kind of deal can you get?" asked Luke.

"With what I have learned here, the best I can get is 3 years, but the worse would be 5," said David.

"Get me the deal," said Luke.

"That's the way you want it to play out then," said David.

"Yes," said Luke.

"OK, I'll have to arrange a time to meet with the district attorney and the judge." "It might take a few days," added David.

Luke looked at his lawyer, "I'm not going anyplace."

Nancy came into the room just before dinner time. "Hi"

"Hi," said Luke back. "Nice to see you."

"Nice to see you," said Nancy with a smile.

"Street clothes!" Looks good on you," he said with a smile.

"Yes, I got off work about an hour ago," she said. "Didn't want some grumpy old orderly feeding my favourite patient."

"Favourite patient, hey," said Luke with a smile.

"So you going to be my official feeder from now on," he said laughing.

"I wouldn't put it quite that way. It sounds too much like a farm hand feeding a horse," she said.

"A horse, now I'm a horse," said Luke a smile on his face and a twinkle in his eyes.

Nancy laughed. "Shut up and eat your oats." She put the first fork full of food close to his mouth for him to take.

"Neigh," he said and took the food.

The rest of the dinner was eaten in silence.

When he was finished he said, "Thanks Nancy."

"My pleasure," said Nancy and leaned over and kissed him on the forehead. Then put the over-bed table to the side and left.

Later an orderly came in and washed him down for the evening and left.

Luke laid there quietly thinking back to the accident. He didn't remember much after reaching the top of the hill. As he laid there remembering a picture came in his mind of motion and silence. He remembered opening his eyes just after the car went airborne. Everything was surreal, he could feel his body pressed against the seat belt as the car started to descend, he saw John his fists digging into the dashboard. There was no sound. He looked forward, his hands clenched on the steering wheel. He saw a car as the nose of the BMW dipped downward. He knew it was his parent's car. That's when he closed his eyes again. That's when sound once again entered his world, the crunching of metal against metal, plastic tearing and glass shattering, screams and air backs pushing against him, silence and tumbling and things breaking and pain.

Luke woke up the next morning from the now familiar voice of Nancy. "Wake up sunshine, time for breakfast."

Luke opened his eyes as Nancy raised the head of the bed. "Back in the work clothes I see."

"Yes, and you have to be on your best behaviour. We are being watched," she said.

"Watched by who," asked Luke.

"I had a meeting with the administrator this morning. It's unprofessional to become 'familiar' with the patients. especially one that is under arrest."

"Wow, what did you say?"

"I just reminded him that I was here as a volunteer and what I did, as long as it didn't affect my work, was none of his business."

"OK and you didn't get kicked out!"

"He just said that he would be watching me and any slip up and I was out of here."

"So that means I get a 10 minute breakfast instead of a 20 minute breakfast," smiled Luke.

"No, it just means that I can't smuggle in files and hacksaw blades," she said with a laugh.

"Oh ya, I'll cut off the cast and the steel holding my legs together and slither out of here."

They both laughed and Nancy tidied up the bed after the breakfast and left.

About a week after David's first visited with Luke, he returned with another man. "Luke this is Mr. Anthony, he is the prosecutor for the DA in this case, and he is here to read out the decision of the judge."

Prison

Mr. Anthony didn't look at Luke, he pulled a document out of his brief case and read, "Luke Dawson you have pleaded guilty to auto theft, reckless driving and 3 counts of vehicle manslaughter. The court has sentenced you to 4 years in a minimum security prison. The court has also arranged for you to attend university to get your computer engineering diploma." "The court has acquired a student loan for you, that you will pay back once you are released from prison and start working."

Mr. Anthony handed the document to David, picked up his brief case and left.

"The District Attorney's office isn't happy with the judge's decision," said David after Mr. Anthony was out of the room. "They wanted 6 years and no schooling."

"Thanks Mr. Ruth, I appreciate what you have done for me," said Luke trying to put out his had to shake David's.

"The doctors tell me that you will have to stay in the hospital for at least another month," said David. "Once you are released from the hospital you will be taken to the Willington Correctional Institution."

"Thanks again," said Luke.

After David left Luke's doctor came into the room. "Well, how are we today, I'm Doctor Smythe," he said as he looked at Luke's legs. "Hmmm, good," he said as he poked and felt different areas on the legs.

"I'm going to schedule surgery to remove the steel pins and put steel plates in your legs to help with the healing process. Once the plates are in place you will be able to start therapy and get you walking in a few weeks."

"That sounds great," said Luke. "What about my arms?"

"We are going to remove the bandages from the right arm this afternoon." "The left arm we are going to check prior to surgery on your legs to see if we can also stabilize it as well."

"OK," said Luke.

Later that day Nancy came in with a nurse and they started to remove the bandage from Luke's right arm.

The nurse looked over the staples in the arm and nodded to Nancy.

Nancy washed the arm with disinfectant and then with warm water and dried the arm with a towel.

"Nice," said Luke looking at the staples in his forearm. "You give good washing, maybe I should keep you," he said teasingly.

Nancy looked at Luke, "I'm a good cook among other things," she said with a wry smile. "I'll see you at dinner time." And she left.

That evening Nancy helped Luke with his dinner. Luke was able to feed himself now that his right arm was bandage free, but opening containers was still a problem.

When finished Luke looked at Nancy and smiled, "thanks."

Nancy moved the over-bed table to a side and sat on the bed. "Luke when I am working, it is all business. I don't want you to flirt with me during that time. Do you understand?"

Luke looked at Nancy a little shocked. "Yes I understand."

"I need this experience at the hospital for future references in nursing school. Besides I might end up working here some day and I want a good track record."

Then Nancy leaned over and kissed Luke on the lips. "When I am off work, that is an entirely different story."

Luke put his arm around her and pulled her close and gave her a kiss back.

Nancy then drew away from him. "Easy big boy," she said with a smile, "you're all broken up, you are in no condition to go any further then a harmless kiss."

"You call that a harmless kiss!" "Wow what is a dangerous kiss like," stammered Luke.

"That you will have to wait 4 years for," said Nancy softly.

"4 years I don't think I could wait that long."

Nancy stroked Luke's neck, "you're going to have to." She lifted the sheet and pointed down to his penis.

"Oh," he said, "I didn't notice that before." Referring to the catheter inserted into him.

"You have a good sleep," said Nancy as she gave him another kiss and left.

Three days later Luke was taken down to radiography for x-rays on his legs and left arm. In the afternoon Dr. Smythe came in and told him the operation was scheduled for the next morning. "Everything looks good," he said, "We can stabilize the arm and both legs with surgical steel plates and pins, which should get you mobile in a few weeks with proper therapy."

Early in the morning Luke was prepared for surgery and wheeled down to the operating room. Once transferred to the operating table, a technician started removing some of the braces on his legs. He felt the technician loosening clamps, then fell asleep.

When he woke up he was in the recovery room. The cast was off his left arm and there were no steel rods sticking out of his legs.

"How do you feel," asked a voice from a distance.

"Thirsty," croaked Luke.

"Here, just a sip though," said the nurse putting a straw to Luke's lips.

Luke took a sip, "that's better. Thanks."

"I'm calling an orderly to take you back to your room," said the nurse as she hurried away to her station to make the call.

Luke laid there for a few minutes and a young man came over and looked at the chart at the foot of the bed. "Luke Dawson, yep got the right one," he said and released the brakes on the bed and pulled it into the hallway.

Luke was still a little groggy from the operation and closed his eyes as the bed was pushed along the corridor past other patients dropped off along the wall waiting for their turn for some medical procedure.

Luke slept most of the day and was happy to see Nancy that evening. He managed to manoeuvre himself through supper and was just finishing up when she came in.

"Look at you, feeding yourself," she said with a smile. "I am sure glad to see that you know how to use a fork and a knife."

Luke laughed, "It's all the good training I got watching you."

"I can't stay long I have an orientation class this evening for school. I'll see you tomorrow." She leaned over gave him a kiss and left.

After breakfast the next morning an orderly came in the room pushing a wheel chair. "Your chariot has arrived dear sir," laughed the orderly. "I'm Paul, your physiotherapist for the next couple weeks."

Luke saw less of Nancy during the day now that he was able to feed himself and generally wash himself in the bed. Now he was almost buddy buddy with Paul, who picked him up for physio twice a day.

Luke's left arm was getting stronger and he was starting to master crutches. He still was limited to the amount of weight he could put on his legs, so it was a struggle getting around.

A week and a half into his therapy a sheriff from the prison where Luke was to serve his sentence walked into the hospital room. "Luke Dawson?" he said looking at Luke.

"Yes," said Luke questioning.

"I wanted to let you know that a transfer order has been issued to have you moved from here to the Willingdon penitentiary hospital tomorrow at noon." "I understand your condition and circumstance," the sheriff added, "and wanted to give you time to prepare for the transfer."

"Thank you," said Luke, "I appreciate the thoughtfulness."

"I'll see you tomorrow at noon," said the sheriff as he left.

Paul picked up Luke for the afternoon session, "I guess this is the last time for us," he said.

"Ya, I'm being moved tomorrow," said Luke.

"There will be a sheriff's deputy outside your door from now until you are moved tomorrow," said Paul.

"A guard what for," said Luke in disbelief. "Do they think I'm going to walk out of here?"

"It's happened before, so they are taking no chances," said Paul.

"They didn't have to do that, but I understand," said Luke resigned to the situation.

That evening when Nancy came to visit she had to report to the guard and have her purse and the bag that she was carrying inspected.

Luke raised the head of the bed so that he was sitting upright by the time she came into the room. "Personal body guard," he said motioning to the guard at the door.

"I noticed," said Nancy. "Here this is for you," she said handing him the bag that was closely inspected by the guard.

In the bag was a razor, tooth brush, tooth paste, a comb, hand soap and shampoo.

"I was thinking of getting you some clothes, but I think that is taken care of for the next few years."

"Thanks," is all Luke could say. He took Nancy's hand and pulled her to him. He kissed her and said, "Thanks," again.

"Stay with me tonight," said Luke softly.

Nancy lay on the bed beside Luke, "I'll stay for awhile," she whispered.

Luke put his arm around her and she snuggled up putting her head on his chest.

The next morning Luke washed up after his breakfast and gathered his toiletries and put them in a plastic bag. Standard prison clothing was supplied and he put those on and waited for Nancy to come in. The sheriff arrived just before lunch.

"I'm sorry Luke but I have to put the handcuffs on you. Its standard procedure," said the sheriff as he took the cuffs and put them on Luke's wrists.

Luke looked around to see if Nancy was coming, but didn't see her. He was glad she didn't show up, because he didn't want her to see him like this.

Luke still couldn't put full wait on his legs so he manoeuvred himself on the bed to get into the waiting wheelchair.

The sheriff pushed Luke out of the room and down the hall to the administration wing. There the sheriff signed some papers and they went out to the waiting van.

Luke was helped into the van and the wheelchair returned to the hospital lobby.

As Luke sat in the van he noticed Nancy out of the corner of his eye. She was standing inside the lobby, looking out one of the side windows. She gave a small wave when she knew that he had seen her. He threw her a kiss and turned away as the van drove away.

Half an hour later the van arrived at the prison and they drove into the inspection bay then drove along a road that had barbwire fencing on both sides. They stopped at a grey door in a grey one storey building that was separate from the regular prison buildings.

The sheriff got out went through the grey door and returned with an old wheelchair.

Luke was helped into it and the sheriff wheeled him into the grey building.

Inside was surprisingly bright. The floor was a light green linoleum, highly polished. The walls were white and the ceiling, white, with rows of fluorescent lights.

The sheriff pushed Luke up to a desk, signed more papers and left. An orderly in prison clothing came up and pushed Luke into one of the rooms.

"This is your room," he said and left.

Luke looked around, "not much," he thought to himself. The room was about 8 feet by 10 feet it had the standard hospital bed, an over-bed table, a closet and a smaller room with a toilet and sink. He later found out that if he wanted a shower he would have to go to the end of the hall to the common shower room.

He was not allowed to leave the room unless accompanied by an orderly, a trustee of the prison.

Luke's physiotherapist was certified and very good at his job. Within a week he was walking with the crutches and putting more weight on his legs.

His physiotherapy workout was also designed to build muscle, being confined to a hospital bed for a couple months left his muscles weak.

Another 4 weeks in the hospital and Luke was walking without the crutches and he was now able to remove the aircasts that he had been wearing for the past 8 weeks.

A week later, Luke was released from the prison hospital and taken to the main prison. Luke walked with his head down not noticing or hearing anything. The guard stopped in front of an open cell. Inside a very big black man stood staring down at him. "This is your new cell mate", said the guard as he pushed Luke in.

Luke stood in the open doorway not knowing what he should do or what was going to happen to him.

"I'm Slade," said the man, in a deep baritone voice. "That's your bunk over there," pointing to a bed in the back of the cell next to the small sink.

Luke quietly walked over to the bed and sat on it, putting his extra clothes and bedding on the bed beside him. He sat there looking at his prison issued shoes. Black and white runners!

He got up put his belongings into the assigned cupboard and made the bed. Tears filled his eyes as he lay down and faced the wall.

Slade sat on his own bed and went back to the book he was reading. His bed was closer to the front of the cell, a couple feet from the bars. Along the wall extending from his bed to the back wall were book shelves, filled with mystery novels, computer technology books and si-fi novels. Along the back wall were a toilet, small sink then Luke's bed. From Luke's bed to the cell bars were more book shelves plus a stereo system and small TV.

Slade left Luke alone for the rest of the day.

At supper time Slade nudged Luke, "Come on, time to eat," he said in his deep baritone voice.

Luke got up and followed Slade like a little puppy to the dining hall.

Once there, Slade motioned Luke to go in front of him at the food counter. "Look at no one and speak to no one," Slade whispered to him as they joined the others lining up for food.

Once their plates were full they walked over to a vacant table and sat down. Luke kept his head down and concentrated on the food in front of him, mashed potatoes, peas and carrots, and some sort of meat..

"Hey Slade, I see you have a new boy." yelled someone from the throng of men sitting at the tables.

Slade only looked up and gave a stern look into open space, then went back to his meal.

After the meal Slade motioned Luke to leave. Luke walked in front of Slade, his head down, eyes focused on his footsteps.

Back at their cell Slade said, "Get some rest kid."

Luke went back to his bed and laid down again, his face against the wall.

In the morning he heard water running.

When he turned he saw Slade washing up in the small sink.

"Freshen up kid, and then I'll give you the rules you have to follow"

Rules, what rules thought Luke.

Luke washed his hands and face and dried them with one of the towels still laying on his bed.

Luke sat on his bed and faced Slade.

Slade looked at him and said "there are three rules you have to follow." "If you don't, you will end up as someone's girl friend by the end of the week."

Luke looked at Slade wondering if he was kidding.

"This is serious, most newbies who come here don't survive the first couple weeks without getting 'blemished'," said Slade.

"1st - you don't go anywhere without me"

"2nd - you enrol in the prison work program for weekend work."

"3rd - you go to the gym and build up your body."

"This 3rd rule is very important. You look like a bean pole. You have to build muscle or you won't last long here."

"I was working out in the hospital," said Luke defensively.

Slade glared at Luke, his eyes squinting, just a narrow slit of eye was showing. "Hospital, They don't have what you need. I'll put you on a training program that will build a man out of you."

Slade continued on his original line of thought, "I'll take care of you for the first year. After that you are on your own."

"Why are you doing this?" asked Luke shaking a bit from the reality check.

"I was asked to get you settled into prison life." said Slade.

"But why did you say yes?"

"Because that's what I do," said Slade looking Luke in the eyes. "I take care of people."

"The reason I am in prison is because I have a very very bad temper. When it gets out I lose all control over my actions and when that happens someone always gets hurt, or even worse … dead."

"OK, so what did you do to get here," asked Luke getting a little braver.

"I was a science teacher, one day I was walking home and I saw 5 men beating a woman. I went up to them and told them to stop and leave. One of them pulled a knife on me and lunged towards me. I grabbed his arm and twisted it until he dropped the knife."

"I'm a big man and I have the strength to go with it," said Slade.

"It turned out that I had twisted his arm so violently that I tore the arm off at the shoulder."

"Before I had time to think another man pulled a gun and shot me in the side. He didn't have a chance to get another shot off before I reached him. I picked him up and slammed him backwards across my knee and threw him 20 feet against a dumpster. He laid there his body bent in half."

I third man ran up as I was dealing with the 2nd man and stabbed me in the side with a knife, just as I was throwing the 2nd man away. I grabbed the third man by the head and twisted it. He fell to the grand, his head facing his back."

"After that I don't remember what happened, but was told that the 4th and 5th men were beaten to death."

"Wow!" said Luke. "It sounds like you were just defending yourself."

Slade looked away from Luke, "It turned out that the woman was a hooker and one of the guys I killed was her pimp and boy friend and they were just disciplining her. Apparently she must have tried to stop me, I don't remember. When I finally calmed down the police where already there and there were six bodies laying on the ground. The woman who I initially tried to save was also dead by my hand."

"I was sentenced to 2 years for manslaughter of the woman, it was deemed self defence for the death of the 5 men. Getting shot and stabbed was the reason for the self defence verdict."

"How long have you been here." asked Luke?

"8 years, I had a little incident here during my first year. One of the inmates wanted to make a name for himself and tried to stab me with a blade. He didn't survive."

"A couple months later 3 men jumped me. I suffered a stab wound to the chest. The three men suffered death."

"For those deaths I was given another 8 years and more anger management therapy."

Luke looked at Slade, "is the anger management working?"

"Not really," said Slade.

"So don't piss me off," he said with a smile.

"What is your story, why are you here?" asked Slade.

"I was working as a valet at one of the hotels downtown. My supervisor and I went for a little ride in a guest's car. I totalled the car and 3 people died in the process."

"So you are the 'flying BMW man'." said Slade.

"The what?"

"Flying BMW man. That's what we call you in here."

"Now I am really going to have to watch out for you. I'm sure some of these guys would love to throw you through the air to see if you could really fly."

"Before the accident," said Luke, "I thought that life was mine for the taking. I thought life was a scenario that if I played my cards rights I could breeze through life and get whatever I wanted. After the accident everything changed. I was no longer master of my own fate. I was no longer in control of my life. Now I am in prison where my every move is watched. My every action is noted down. My life is in someone else's hands. At times I think I might go crazy. Then I think of the life I lost and the possibility of getting that life back."

Luke looked at Slade with hope in his eyes. "That is why I am going to work hard to get my computer engineer degree. I want to see how far I can push the limits of this technology. How I can manipulate the code to get the most out of the computer. I have discovered that the computer is limited only by the imagination of the operator. It isn't speed of processing or the size of the memory; it is what can be accomplished within those boundaries. In the computer I know that I am in control of my life. Through computers I am master of my life. I am discovering that I can do anything with computers. These walls of steel and concrete cannot hold me in. This technology is my spirituality. My mantra. My salvation."

Slade looked at Luke and shook his head. "You may be master of your computer, but you are living in a dream world. You're naive about what goes on in real life. Life is a constant struggle. You may think you are in control but you aren't. The minute you think everything is rosy something happens and you discover how helpless you are. Life is like that good at times, better at other times and terrible most of the times."

"Look at me," said Slade. "I was an honest person never ever got into trouble. Respected in the community. Then one day I try to help someone in need and find out that I have an alter ego .... One that likes to hurt people."

"So you never know kid what life will throw at you."

"What can happen?" asked Luke. "In here"

"There are certain men in here that have acquired control and dominance over most of the inmates." Said Slade with a serious look on his face. "Many attempts have been made to try to get to me, but I have been able to maintain my freedom from them."

"In here anything can happen and no one will care about the victim, because they don't want to be that victim. You will be challenged. How you handle it will mean life or death to you. If you fight it or try to resist, you will fail. If you go along with it, even though you don't agree with it, you will survive. But when you play your roll and you want out it will be very difficult. Even getting out of here won't free you from the pressures within these walls. The only way to break free from oppression is to make sure the source of that oppression no long exists."

Slade looked at Luke hard and long, "there is a saying within these walls that is very true here and on the outside." Slade said so softly that Luke could hardly here him, "revenge is best served cold."

"These are the hard facts of life in prison kid. You will be tested. It's up to you how you handle it."

Luke sat on his bed listening to Slade and wondered how he would handle such a situation.

The next day after breakfast instead of returning to their cell Slade steered Luke to the gym. "Time to start you on a weight training program," said Slade as he swung the doors open to the gym.

Immediately the smell of sweat and stale air hit Luke's nostrils. He looked around and there were three men already in the gym working out.

"We'll start with what you can do and work from there," said Slade taking Luke over to the bench press area.

Luke did a few presses with 125 pounds, then went to the other stations and did a few reps at each.

"Not bad," said Slate. "You have a good base to work on." Slade wrote down a program for Luke to follow and watched him as he went through the stations and doing the workout that was written on the schedule. As Luke did his exercises Slade also worked out behind him.

Luke would do a rep at a station, then while he rested before the next rep Slade did a rep.

Luke stood in awe as he saw Slade load the weights on the bar at the bench press. Luke added up 500 lbs. on the bar and Slade pressed it easier then Luke had pressed the 125 lbs.

After going through the work out Luke was exhausted.

Slade and Luke went in the shower, "not bad kid," said Slade washing the perspiration from his body.

"We'll do this every day," said Slade. "When you start school, we'll do this in the evening when you get back."

Luke started school a week later. Slade escorted him to the guard's station, "I'll be here when you get back. If I'm not here wait for me."

"I'm not a little kid," said Luke.

"Wait for me," said Slade in a stern voice.

Luke shuddered a bit, "OK."

When Luke came back Slade was at the guard station talking with one of the guards.

Luke and Slade walked back to their cell without talking. Once there Slade asked, "How was your first day?"

"It went well," said Luke. "I got a few glares from other students when I drove up in the prison van. But it's cool."

"Workout time before dinner," said Slade grabbing his gym equipment.

Luke wanted to just lay down and rest. "Can we leave it 'til later," he begged.

"Nope. If you start that you will never have the energy or the mental alertness to work after dinner," said Slade.

"OK," said Luke dragging himself off the bed and grabbing his workout clothes.

This was the routine for the next few weeks. Luke actually started to look forward to his workout after school.

One day when Luke got back to the prison after school, Slade wasn't there waiting for him. Luke looked at the guard, "where is Slade?"

The guard shrugged his shoulders, "I don't know."

Luke stayed with the guard and about fifteen minutes later Slade came, "I was held up a bit," is all he said.

Luke and Slade walked to the door separating the guard's station from the prison corridor. The electronic buzz told them the door had been unlocked and they went through into the main corridor. This corridor was different from the other prison corridors. This one was a connection from the entrance guard station, where visitors and students entered. This corridor led to the visitor's room as well as the main prison area. At the end of the corridor was another locked door controlled by the station on the other side. The visitor's room door was half way down the corridor and was also locked. A guard would escort the visitor to the door, unlock it and then lock it again once the visitor was inside. To make it easier on the visitors the walls of the corridor were painted a light green and the concrete floor was painted brown. The ceiling had standard ceiling tiles.

Once out of site of the guards Slade stopped and held out his hand. In it was a piece of steel sharpened and tape wrapped around one end for a handle. "I have to get rid of this," he said, looking at the make-shift knife. "The guards won't check you, so hid it."

Luke took the knife and held it in his hand. He carefully checked how it balanced and its weight. Then he looked up at the high ceiling in the hallway. The ceiling was 12 feet high and had white ceiling tiles lining it. Fluorescent light fixtures ran along the center of the ceiling from one end to the other. Where the light fixtures met the ceiling tiles there was a small gap.

Luke looked over at Slade then looked up. With a flick of his arm Luke threw the knife upward and it disappeared between the light fixture and the ceiling tiles landing somewhere above the ceiling.

"Lucky throw," said Slade.

"No luck involved," said Luke. "My hobby was knife throwing. My mom would get angry with me because I would take all the steak knives from the kitchen and go into the garage and use them to practise with. I would throw them at a cork board I had set up and see what kind of patterns I could make. I would pick out a specific spot on the board and throw the knife to land at that spot. I got very good at it."

Slade shook his head in amazement and started walking again. They came to the door at the end of the corridor and buzzed for the guard to unlock it. They went through the open door, ahead of them were 5 guards talking to a few of the prisoners. One of them was in obvious pain.

"Don't say anything," whispered Slade.

They walked past the prisoners and guards and Luke saw the man that was in pain, his right hand crushed and hanging limp at the end of his arm.

"Slade," said one of the guards, "you know anything about this?"

Slade looked at the injured man, then at the other prisoners standing around. "Haven't a clue," he said.

The guard looked at Slade then Luke, "Slade against the wall," said the guard.

Slade moved to the wall and faced it and put his hands above his head and against the wall.

"Frisk him," said the guard to another guard.

The other guard checked Slade for any prohibited items that might be hidden in his clothing.

"Nothing," said the guard.

"Check the other one," said the head guard pointing at Luke.

Luke took off his back pack and stood against the wall.

The guard checked him out then went through his back pack. Satisfied the guard looked at Slade and Luke, "Get going."

In their cell Luke asked, "What was that all about?"

Slade put his finger to his lips, "Shhhh."

Slade then sat on Luke's bed with his back to the door. "That guy attacked me on my way to meet you," said Slade in a whisper. "He had a blade, luckily I noticed him before he could cut me. When I took the blade from him his hand sort of got damaged. Then I had to get rid of the blade before the guards came."

"Why did he want to hurt you?" asked Luke.

"His boss wanted me out of the way so that he could get to you," said Slade.

"Me, what for?" shouted Luke.

"Shhhh. Keep quiet. We are being listened to," said Slade pointing to the speakers mounted in the ceiling just outside their cell. "Those are a two way speaker / microphone system. They hear everything we say."

"OK, that's why the whispering," said Luke.

Slade nodded his head.

"What does he want with me?" Luke asked again softly.

"There is one person in this prison who has control over most of the population. He has this control by having information on each and every one of them that could be very harmful to them or a loved one. Usually a loved one," said Slade.

"I'll have a talk with him and have him back off for now," continued Slade. "Stay here."

Slade left and walked towards the courtyard. The courtyard was a concrete rectangle in the middle of the prison. At one end were the administration offices. Its brick wall faced the courtyard and one of the two basketball courts. At the opposite end was the hospital with the other basketball court. On each side running along the longest side of the courtyard were the prisons themselves. On one side were minor offences and short term inmates. On the other side was for longer terms and serious offences where Luke was.

"Johnson, a word," called Slade when he saw the guy he was looking for sitting on one of the benches.

"Why Slade, my good friend," said Johnson, a big smile on his face.

"Luke is mine for the rest of the year. You try another stunt like today and certain secrets will be told," said Slade looking Johnson square in the eyes. "Do you understand me?"

Johnson, his smile gone for a second, "Sure Slade, I understand."

Slade turned and walked back the way he had come.

"Workout time kid," said Slade when he got back.

Luke picked up his gym clothes and followed Slade to the gym.

After dinner and back in their cell Luke asked Slade what he did.

Slade sat on Luke's bed again his back to the cell door.

"Two years ago I was given a new arrival to initiate into prison life," said Slade. "This new guy's name was Johnson, the same guy who wants to get to you. Anyway back then we had a bat problem in the prison. They would find their way inside the cell area sometimes. One night shortly after Johnson arrived a bat found its way into out cell. Johnson freaked out and before I could catch the bat Johnson had become almost catatonic with fear."

"It turned out that Johnson was deathly afraid of bats and he requested that I tell no one," said Slade. "You are the only one I have told this to."

"Three days later he had found out that someone had thrown the bat into our cell. It was no accident," said Slade. "Johnson found out who it was and carefully planned his revenge. The guy was found dead in his cell. There was an inquiry, but no one was charged with the incident."

"A few days later Johnson requested transfer to a different cell, and he has been seeking control of everyone every since."

"Wow," said Luke. "So he wants me …. Why?"

"Probably to get information for him," whispered Slade. "Computers aren't readily available in prison and there is no internet access, other than the inmate computer room, which is monitored constantly."

"You're safe for now, as long as you are with me," reminded Slade.

On the weekends Nancy would come and visit Luke. They talked about their classes and Nancy would talk about things on the outside. Luke never mentioned what was going on inside the prison other then mentioning his workout routine with Slade.

"Yes, I noticed," said Nancy with a little tune in her voice. "Looking gooood."

"I met a nice couple at the university, Tom and Judy," Nancy said one day on their regular weekend visits. "I was having some problems with a couple of the other students harassing me to go out with them, but Tom stepped in and told them to back off. Tom makes sure that I am safe. He and Judy walk me to and from classes. It's wonderful."

"I'm glad you're safe," said Luke feeling angry that he wasn't there to protect her.

"Are you off for the summer?" asked Luke.

"One week then I'm back at it," said Nancy. "I want to get my nursing degree as fast as possible. So I'm starting my second year right away."

"I have 2 weeks off before my second year starts," said Luke. "I think Slade has me booked for some project during that time."

"Well good luck," said Nancy. "I'll see you in 2 weeks."

"OK," said Luke, kissing her good bye.

Luke walked out of the visitor's room and Slade was waiting for him. "You ready to work!" he said.

"I guess," said Luke.

"Good, come with me." Slade headed off in the direction of the administration office then turned right, down a corridor Luke had never been down before. This corridor was obviously off limits to the main prison population. The walls were brightly painted with posters and artwork on the walls.

"Where you taking me?" asked Luke.

"You'll see," said Slade with a big smile on his face.

At the end of the corridor were two locked doors. Slade took a key out of his pocket and unlocked the door on the right. Through the door there were steps that led to the roof. "Up you go," said Slade.

"Where does that go?" questioned Luke pointing to the other door.

"The guard's changing rooms," said Luke pointing for Luke to go up the stairs.

On the roof Luke could see the entire courtyard as well as the nearby town with its houses and parks. Luke looked at Slade questioning.

"Every year on July 4th all the inmates of the prison as well as the guards come up here and watch the fireworks display from the town. In return we put on a light show for them. This year we get to design and build the display," said Slade.

"Wow," said Luke. "What kind of theme did you have in mind?"

"I want a huge flag 10 feet high that waves as though it is in the wind and lights that resemble rockets shooting skyward," said Slade dramatizing his description with his hands.

"That's a big undertaking," said Luke.

"Can you get all that built in 11 days?" asked Slade.

"Eleven days! That's a tall order. I'll need internet access, a really good computer and privacy," said Luke.

"I have that all arranged," said Slade, "Can you get the computer program for the lighting done in 2 days?"

"What? You want me to create a program for the lighting?"

"Yep, exactly like I described it to you," said Slade. "I've arranged a place to set up a small scale model of what I want. You can work on your program there also. I'll arrange to have the number of light strings and colors available before you finish. You have 2 days, and then we will have a few days to install the real thing."

Slade took a few measurements and went down the stairs, Luke in tow. They went to the inmate computer room, walked past work stations to the back of the room. Slade unlocked the door to a small storage room. This is your design room for the project. Already set up were the scaled down version of the flag and a couple strings of lights representing the rockets.

"Good luck," said Slade as he closed the door behind him leaving Luke in the room.

On the desk were a laptop computer and a few of Luke's books and a couple other books that he had noticed in the book shelves in Slade's section of the cell. He sat down and started making the tree diagram layout for the project.

The programming for the sequence of lights turning off and on was readily available. It had already been written for some of the super bowl half time shows, and the rocket display was also available. The only thing was to change a few variables for size and number of lights, then save it on a flash drive and test it.

Luke configured the test for the scale model and inserted the flash drive into the light controller port, then turned it on.

At that moment Slade walked in and saw the lights dancing. He walked over to the DVD player and inserted a disc. The music to 'Star Spangled Banner' by Jimi Hendrix started to play and the lights danced in tune to the music. "Excellent," said Slade. "Now we'll construct the real display. Will the program work for it?"

"Yes," said Luke rubbing his ears. "I just have to input the size and number of lights."

"Good, good!" "Let's get started," said Slade all giddy.

On the fourth of July, a special dinner was prepared. Afterwards the inmates proceeded to the roof of the cell block to watch the fireworks display put on by the town council. Luke was with Slade at the base of their construction. Luke watched as the inmates came up the stairs. Each proceeded to a specific spot, their spot, on the roof.

"How long has this 4th of July celebration been going on at the prison?" asked Luke.

"Ever since the prison opened, there have been inmates watching from this roof," said Slade.

Luke kept on watching as more inmates found their 'spot'. Johnson was one of the last inmates to reach the roof, followed by the guards. Johnson walked to the very front next to a concrete railing support. The guards also had their 'spots' and stood there on the perimeter of the congregation.

From Luke's position under the display and at the main controls he had an unobstructed view of Johnson and the area where the fireworks were going to be displayed in the town. Also looking around he couldn't see any of the guards.

The fireworks display started and for an hour everyone 'oooed' and 'awwwed' at the magnificent bursts of lights in the sky.

Then it was the prison inmates turn to reciprocate in the delights. Everyone turned around to look at the 10 foot tall structure on the very back edge of the roof. Luke threw the switch to the on position. To the tune of Jimi Hendrix doing the 'Star Spangled Banner' the lights shone brightly in the form of the flag waving in the wind and rockets shooting 20 feet into the air.

For five minutes the music played and the lights danced, then it was over. From the town could be heard a horn blowing, indicating their delight and approval of the show.

Luke was transferred to another section of the prison a week later, and he started his second year of college. His new cell mate was an older man, in his mid 60's. He had been in prison for 6 years on the charge of embezzlement at the bank he worked at. He was due for release in another year.

During the second month of college, Johnson approached him when he got back to the prison.

"We need to talk," said Johnson quietly as he walked pass Luke and motioned him to follow.

"What do you want?" asked Luke when they entered the courtyard.

"Nothing much," said Johnson, "just information."

"There are a few men in here that are not, how can I say this … not on the same page as I am, and I don't like it."

"I want you to get information from the prison files on these men and give it to me."

"And how am I suppose to do that?" asked Luke.

"I'll tell you how. You are going to hack into the main computer and get the files."

"Impossible," said Luke. "There is no link between the prison computers and the prison main computer."

"I know that," said Johnson. "That's why I have chosen you."

"I have been getting regular reports on how good you are with computers. I'm sure you can figure a way of getting what I want." Johnson smiled a wry smile and awaited Luke's response.

"It can't be done. Not by me, anyways" said Luke. "I haven't completed the hacker's course yet."

"Don't get smart with me, boy," snarled Johnson. "You will get the information I want."

"What makes you think, I will cooperate with you?"

"By being a good boy and wanting to protect that fine young lady friend of yours." Johnson gave that wry smile again, the corners of his mouth rising upward, lips closed.

Luke looked at Johnson, "you leave Nancy alone." Luke took a step towards Johnson and one of the men with them stepped in and grabbed Luke.

Johnson very quietly said, "That friend of Nancy's, Tom. His father is an inmate here, and I control him, and if he tells Tom to do something, Tom will do it."

"You bastard," said Luke.

"Hack into the prison computer," said Johnson and Nancy will be safe. He then turned away from Luke and strutted towards the cell block.

Luke thought about Nancy and on the weekend when she came to visit, he made sure that he didn't sound or act like anything was wrong.

Nursing school was going good and Tom and Judy where always around to keep her company.

On the Monday Luke watched especially closely when the guard signed him in after the day at the college. He noticed that the guard needed a password to login when he entered the time and date of Luke returning to the prison. From his side of the entry door standing close to the door he couldn't see what was entered but if he moved over a bit away from the door he had a clear view of the keyboard.

The next day Luke struck up a conversation with the guard that always picked him up from the college, and stood in a position where he could see the keyboard through the window in the admittance office. Now all he had to do was hack into the prison computer …. Easier said than done. His internet access was monitored at the school, part of the conditions set up for him to attend school, and there was no internet access in the prison. That left him with the 15 minute ride from the school to the prison, and then he was watched.

Each day he would spend the 15 minute ride on his lap top trying to hack into the prison computer. Finally on the 4th day he was successful in getting access to the prison computer. The administration computer did not have a direct link to the server that was used by the guards. After searching around inside the administration computer he found an external link that would take him to the server that the guards used.

The next day on his ride to the prison he entered the link and when asked for the user and password, he entered the user name used by the guard and the password. He got an error message saying that the IP addresses did not match and access was denied.

On his return to prison, Luke went into the courtyard to find Johnson. "I have some bad news," he said when he found Johnson sitting on one of the benches. "The server the guards use has a computer identity recognition set on it. If access is attempted from a computer other than the one originally set up to the user and password, access is denied."

"Well, that's not my problem is it," said Johnson. "You'll just have to find another way in."

"I am working on another way in," said Luke, "it's going to take a few weeks. Basically I'll hack into the computer used by the guards and through their terminal I will be able to access the server."

"That doesn't sound too difficult," said Johnson.

"It isn't," said Luke. "The hard part is getting into the guard's computer when it isn't being used, after midnight."

"So do it," said Johnson impatiently.

"I have to have an internet connection," said Luke, "and I don't have that connection in here."

"What would it take to get connected?" asked Johnson.

"I need a remote satellite flash drive," said Luke. "It will take a few weeks to get one. I have a friend at school that can get me one at a price."

"Just get me my information," growled Johnson. "I'm getting tired of your excuses. Maybe Nancy needs a little accident. I'm sure you would work faster then."

"Hurting Nancy won't get the information any faster," said Luke. "If this is rushed mistakes will be made and if I get caught, you will never get the information you want."

"You'll have your information by Thanksgiving," added Luke.

Johnson motioned to his accompanying inmates and they walked up to Luke and surrounded him. Johnson looked Luke square in the face. At the same time one of the inmates punched Luke in the kidney area. "By thanksgiving," said

Johnson and the group walked away leaving Luke slumped over in the courtyard.

A few weeks later Luke got the satellite flash drive from his friend and inserted it into the USB port of his computer. The guards always searched him and his back pack, never his computer.

That afternoon Luke was picked up as usual from school and driven to the prison. There the guards did their usual search. Luke put the lap top computer, with the flash drive in the USB port, on the inspection desk along with his back pack.

The guards checked the contents of the backpack and patted down Luke and inspected his shoes. "He's clean," said one of the guards and Luke put his shoes on and picked up the backpack and lap top and walked into the main prison area.

That evening Luke worked on his school project. He knew that the guards were paying close attention to what he was doing. Lights out at 10:00 and Luke closed the lap top but did not sign off. About midnight Luke grabbed the lap top and pulled it under the blanket with him.

With a few key strokes he was in the admittance office computer and logged into the prison main computer where all the information on the inmates was located. He quickly found what he wanted and wrote down the information. To make it easier to get into the computer at any time he set up a backdoor access with a new password that was not based on the IP address of the computer.

The next day, Saturday, Luke did his usual weekend work detail and was looking forward to visiting with Nancy.

Before visiting hours Luke sought out Johnson. In the courtyard Luke looked at Johnson who was sitting at his usual bench and he nodded to him.

Johnson got up and walked towards Luke. Luke did the same thing but looked off towards the other end of the courtyard. As they passed Luke passed the piece of pager to Johnson and kept walking until he met up with Slade who happened to be in the courtyard.

"How is the newbie?" asked Luke, looking at the young man at Slade's side.

"Doing good, not as naive as you were," said Slade with a smile. Then he nodded once and walked away, his charge in tow.

Luke went to the visitor's area and met up with Nancy. "How are things going?" he asked.

Nancy gave Luke a big hug and kissed him, "fine," she said. "Everything is fine."

They visited for about an hour. Luke and Nancy kissed good bye, "till next Saturday" said Nance.

Luke returned to his cell and continued working on his school project. Johnson walked past his cell and tossed a crumpled piece of paper at him, and continued to walk down the corridor.

Luke discretely picked up the wad of paper. Luke had set up a small desk so that he was facing the cell door and his computer away from the surveillance camera. This way they couldn't see what was on his computer screen. Luke opened the note and placed it on the desk in front of the laptop. It was the name of another inmate that Johnson wanted him to get information on.

Luke put the remote internet flash stick into the computer and accessed the prison computer through the back door that he had set up. He quickly found the name he was looking for and wrote the information on the back of the paper that Johnson had thrown into his cell, and crumpled it up and threw it in his trash can.

Minutes later Johnson came back pushing a large garbage bin and was emptying all the trash cans from the cells. When he got to Luke's cell, Luke nodded towards the trash can. Johnson picked up the can, retrieved the crumpled piece of paper and put it in his pocket. The rest of the trash went into the large bin.

Luke realized that Johnson was going to keep this up for the entire time he was in prison and might even find a way to make sure he stayed in prison a bit longer.

Luke closed his laptop and walked out of the cell and down the corridor. "Anderson," he said as he approached one of the inmates. Luke looked up at the speaker-microphone in the ceiling of the corridor and motioned Anderson to follow him. In an area that was far enough away from the speaker-microphones Luke stopped and waited for Anderson to arrive.

"What do you want?" asked Anderson.

"I just gave Johnson some information on you," said Luke. "I told him that you are in here because you beat a person unconscious and that your wife is in the hospital."

"That bastard Johnson," said Anderson. "He's gotten to you too."

"So you told him I beat my wife unconscious," asked Anderson.

"No, I told him you beat someone unconscious, and that your wife was in the hospital," said Luke.

"Oh," smiled Anderson. "My poor wife is in the hospital and the reason I'm in here is because I beat someone unconscious."

"Yes," said Luke. "Whatever I can do to throw that bastard a curve ball, I'll do."

"Thanks for the heads up," said Anderson.

Luke went back to his cell and started to work on a special project, a hologram display for the 4th of July celebrations. He didn't have time to get it done for that year's celebration that was a month away, but would be ready for the following year.

Anderson went out to the courtyard to get some exercise and maybe see Johnson. As soon as he entered the courtyard Johnson saw him and approached him.

"Anderson," said Johnson with an air of superiority, "I have a job for you."

"Not interested," said Anderson as he started to walk away.

"It would be a pity if that lovely wife of yours had a turn for the worse in the hospital," egged Johnson.

"Ya, it would be," said Anderson, stopping and turning towards Johnson.

"If you do this small job for me, I'm sure your wife will be fine," smiled Johnson.

"Not interested," said Anderson. "I don't like being in prison and I'm not going to do anything that will prolong my stay here."

"We will see what you have to say in a couple days," said Johnson sternly.

Anderson continued to walk away from Johnson and towards the far end of the courtyard.

Johnson got a hold of one of the inmates that he 'controlled' and told him to tell someone on the outside to look up Mrs. Anderson in the hospital.

A few days later Anderson got a message from his anger management councillor that one of the machines that his wife was hooked up to malfunctioned. The nurse on duty saw that the machine wasn't working and hooked her up to a backup machine.

The next day Anderson was in the courtyard, Johnson walked up to him. "Sorry to hear about the unfortunate malfunction of that machine your wife is hooked up to."

"Maybe now you will do that small job for me," snickered Johnson.

"I told you before," said Anderson, "I will not work for you."

Johnson glared at Anderson. "The next time your wife might not be so lucky. Maybe she will suffer permanent damage."

Anderson looked at Johnson and laughed a deep bellowing laugh that could be heard through the entire courtyard. "Go fuck yourself." He turned and walked away.

Johnson was furious; no one had ever refused him before. He sent a message out that Anderson's wife was to have a serious accident.

Johnson was hoping that would bring Anderson in line. If he couldn't control Anderson then he would have to have him killed.

A few days later Anderson was informed that his wife had a serious accident in the hospital and she died as a result.

Anderson asked for permission to attend his wife's funeral. His record for the time he was in prison was studied and since he was attending all his therapy sessions and hadn't caused any trouble he was given a day pass, accompanied by a sheriff's deputy.

After the funeral, Anderson went up to Johnson in the courtyard and looked him straight in the eye. "Thank you," he said with a smile and walked off.

Johnson stood in the courtyard his mouth open wondering what just happened. He looked around to see if Luke was in the yard. Then he quickly walked, almost to a run, into the prison and went to Luke's cell. "Come with me," he said walking back the way he came.

"What kind of information you giving me?" stormed Johnson, after they were back in the courtyard.

"The information you asked for," said Luke, knowing what Johnson was referring to. "I was just checking on Anderson's file and there was a section that I had originally missed."

"Oh," said Johnson.

Luke lowered his voice and said, "It seems that Anderson is the one who put his wife in the hospital, she is the person he beat unconscious."

Johnson's face went red, holding in the outburst that was welling up inside him. Controlled he said "that better not happen again," and walked over to his bench and sat down.

The 4th of July had finally arrived and everyone filed onto the roof to watch the fireworks from the town and their own display. One of the other inmates had the honour of presenting the display.

It was good, but not as good as the one that Luke and Slade had put on the year before.

A couple days later Luke asked to see the warden.

"Warden," said Luke, "I would like to conduct the 4th of July display for the prison next year. I have been working on some holographic displays at school and think they would be an excellent medium for a dynamic show."

"We are meeting this evening, but I'm sure you are the favourite choice," said the warden.

The next day Slade and his cell mate met Luke after school. "The decision about the 4th of July display came down today," said Slade. "They want us," pointing to Luke and himself, "to put on the display."

Luke beamed with delight. "That's great; I have a great plan for next year."

"Good," said Slade, "because I don't know how we are going to better the performance we had the last time."

"You've heard of holograms!" said Luke.

"Yes, but that is way out of our league," said Slade.

"Nope," said Luke confidently. "Got it all planned out. I am able to borrow the equipment from the college."

"How did you manage that?" asked Slade.

"Just a little compensation for an anti-hack program I developed," smiled Luke.

"When is it arriving, we have to try it out and see how it looks," said Slade.

"It will be here on the 3rd of July," said Luke.

"That's not enough time to set it up and work out the kinks," said Slade.

"It's all in the programming," said Luke. "I'll have the main program for the entire show finished well before the 4th. We can run a computer simulation and see how it looks. Any adjustments can be done on the computer until we get it to look and sound the way we want…… it will be spectacular."

"OK," said Slade shaking his head in disbelief.

Slade walked off with his charge in tow and headed towards the gym.

As soon as Slade was out of site, Johnson came around a corner and approached Luke.

"I have another person I want information on," whispered Johnson handing a piece of paper to Luke.

Luke took the paper and put it in his pocket. "It will be awhile before I can get this information for you."

"No …. I want the information tomorrow," whispered Johnson sternly.

"Impossible," said Luke. "A few days ago I installed my anti-hacking program on the prison computer. The warden has his people monitoring the computers 24 hours a day watching for any potential hackers trying to get into the system. I can't risk going in right now."

"Well when can I get this info?" asked Johnson.

"Things should ease up somewhat in a few weeks. I can get your information by the end of August."

"I think that pretty little woman of yours might have an accident," snarled Johnson.

"You have her hurt," said Luke, "and you will never get any information from me again. I'll have your information the end of August."

"I'll let my people know to be ready to go into action if there are any more delays," said Johnson, obviously very unhappy about the stoppage of the flow of information.

Luke went back to his cell to work on the programming for the show he wanted to put on for the 4th of July.

He still was able to connect to the internet and searched for the appropriate music video for the show. He quickly found what he wanted and downloaded 'James Brown's Living in America' YouTube video. Then he searched for fireworks displays and found several good video's showing lots of fireworks and some with rockets shooting high in the sky and exploding.

After downloading all the videos that he was going to use, he started to compile his computer program and inserted the music and the fireworks scenes where he wanted them. For each scene he would project the images through the hologram instruments, one scene would be from one hologram and the same scene would be from a second hologram, but only a millisecond behind the first. This would give the hologram a deeper and more vibrant 3D effect. At the appropriate time fireworks would shoot up from a different hologram and yet another hologram would be for the rockets.

In between his school work and the hologram display, Luke acquired the information Johnson wanted and gave it to him on the last day of August.

Johnson immediately handed Luke another name to get information on.

Johnson was still furious about Anderson and was now planning an accident for him.

Anderson was called into the meeting room the end of October, it was a parole hearing and he was granted parole effective in 2 days.

Johnson found out about the parole a day later and had no time to arrange a hit on Anderson; he was livid and vowed to get Anderson one way or another. He searched his records to see who on the outside he could get to 'dispose' of Anderson.

A couple days later Johnson approached Luke for the information on his latest target. Luke handed him a piece of paper with the information and kept walking away from him.

Johnson's requests for information became fewer as Christmas approached. Mainly because he had something on everyone in the prison and there were no new arrivals.

Luke finished the program and called a nervous Slade over to view the show.

Luke began the simulation and Slade stood staring at the computer monitor in awe. In perfect unity the fireworks would be displayed at the same instant that the fireworks in the James Brown video was displayed. Then during the final seconds of the song the fireworks and the rockets exploded into the air showing a display of light that could be seen for tens of miles away. Then finally when the song was finished, five jets ejecting smoke would soar straight up from the roof and peeling off in a blaze of sound that was so loud you would swear they were real jets flying over head.

Luke looked at Slade, "now image that happening over your head 500 feet in height and a thousand feet wide, with the volume up so loud that it would drown out a jet engine."

Slade looked at Luke, "it's crazy …. I love it."

On the 3rd of July the equipment arrived and Luke, Slade and the new inmate started setting it up on the roof of the prison. Unlike the show put on the previous year, Luke set this equipment up as far back on the roof as possible so the full impact of the show could be seen and felt by everyone.

"OK," said Luke, "these two holograms go in the middle, they are for the James Brown video, then two more on either side for the fireworks, rockets and jets."

"This small one," asked Slade, "what is it for?"

"That's the link between the computer and the feedback system to make sure the timing is correct," lied Luke.

The evening of July 4th the inmates were all assembled and watched the fireworks display put on by the town. It was beautiful and more elaborate than any previous year's performance. When they were finished, Luke turned the power on for holograms and instantly an eerie glow appeared in the sky above them. Then Luke turned on the computer and started the program.

Starting 50 feet above their heads a towering 500 foot James Brown started singing his version of 'Living in America', and as promised the music boomed out of four large speakers positioned along the far roof line.

It was a spectacular site seeing the music video and the fireworks and the rockets.

Half way through the show Luke looked down to the assembled inmates. Johnson was in his usual spot, one of his 'soldiers' was at his side.

Luke took the small hologram, the one he told Slade was the link between the computer and the feedback system, and with a lazar aligned the machine up so that it was facing Johnson. Luke had hooked up his old prison computer to the hologram and now started the 'special' program. From the hologram a small black dot appeared surrounded by a bright white light.

Johnson instantly noticed the bright light when Luke turned it on. The black dot got large and appeared to be getting closer to Johnson.

Johnson watched as the black dot got bigger and closer. As the object got bigger the white light faded until there was just a silhouette of something black approaching him. Then he saw what it was. "Aaaaaaaaaaaaa," screamed Johnson, "a bat". He lurched backwards and stumbled over the low roof wall and fell thirty feet to the concrete courtyard below.

Luke turned off the small hologram and disconnected the computer and put it in his backpack, then continued to watch the show as rockets blasted upward and exploded in a loud thunderous roll. It was timed perfectly; the small bat hologram was immediately followed by the rockets. No one but Johnson saw the 'bat', only the rockets souring skyward.

The man that was beside Johnson looked down to the courtyard and saw Johnson laying there, one leg bent under him. The man quietly worked his way past the other inmates and once at the stairs ran down them to the courtyard. He ran over to Johnson and checked if he was alive or dead. He was still alive but had severe injuries. The man grabbed Johnson's head with both hands and lifted it off the concrete floor, then with one quick swift motion slammed Johnson's head into the concrete as hard as he could.

Then the man got up and ran into the cell block. A few minutes later he came back and checked on Johnson. Blood was oozing from his head and there was no pulse to be detected. The man then went back up the stairs to the roof and eased his way back to his spot. But instead of standing close to the edge of the roof, he stood a few steps further on the roof and watched the Jets soaring overhead. Trailing smoke one could hear the straining whine of the jet engines as the holographic planes climbed straight up and peeled off in a flower formation.

When the show was over everyone cheered and yelled at the excellent performance. From the town there was no sounding of the usual horn to show their approval, instead they could hear the yelling and cheering from the townsfolk in a display of shear enjoyment and wonder.

The guards then took their spots at the top of the stairs and took note of everyone heading back to the cell block. "Hey, did you see Johnson," one of the guards asked the guard across from him.

"No, I didn't," said the other guard.

They checked the roof and didn't find him. Then they went down to the courtyard after they heard yelling coming from there.

When they got to the courtyard they say Johnson laying on his back, dead.

The guards immediately instructed the inmates to go to their cells and stay there. Then they notified the warden that Johnson was dead and went to his cell.

Johnson's cell mate, Perry, went to the cell after Johnson was discovered in the courtyard as instructed. The guards came a few minutes later and searched the cell. They new Johnson had a stash of papers someplace in the cell but were never able to find them on routine cell inspections. They moved Perry to another cell and thoroughly searched Johnson's cell removing everything and opening boxes and even checking the mattress. They found nothing.

Whatever information Johnson had, Perry had found the hiding place and took all the papers and stuffed them in his shirt before he returned to the 4th of July display.

The next day Perry went to the laundry room, where he worked, and threw a large amount of paper into the bleaching machine. With a smile on his face he turned on the machine waited a few minutes then turned it off and opened it up. Inside was a mash of paper pulp and a blue tinge to the liquid. Perry notified the guard in the laundry room that the bleach machine needed to be cleaned out and that he would need special equipment to do the job. He drained the bleach and paper mash from the machine and put it all in a 45 gallon drum and sent it out to be disposed of.

Three days later all the inmates were questioned on whether they had seen anything. Everyone said they hadn't. Perry was question and he said that he had not notice Johnson's absence because he was mesmerized by the show.

In the end the incident was classified as an accident and closed.

On the Saturday Luke met Nancy in the visitor's room. Luke told Nancy of the 'accident'.

"It's strange," said Nancy, "yesterday Tom wasn't at school, and this morning I heard that he quit school to go study back East. Judy said he had always talked about studying in New

York. She said that she was going to join him once she finished school this year."

"That was very sudden of him to leave like that," said Luke with a satisfied look on his face.

"Yes," said Nancy.

Nothing more was ever said about the sudden disappearance of Tom.

The following week Luke had his final exams, and the week after that he was granted a parole and was released from prison.

In August Luke now a free man started working for an IT company.

A New Beginning

Luke didn't return to his parent's house. His lawyer said the house was rented to a nice family and they would like to remain in the house. The lawyer also said that all the personal belongings were stored in a trunk in the garage.

Luke rented a truck and drove up to the house and parked on the street. He sat in the truck for a long time thinking of that tragic day almost four years ago.

He wiped his face and walked up to the front door of the house.

"I'm Luke Dawson," he said when a man opened the door.

"Yes, the lawyer said you were coming over," said the man. "I'm John, Come in."

Luke walked into the house and looked around. All of his parent's furniture was still there. The house was rented fully furnished. Luke walked to the garage door and opened it and walked in.

"That's your trunk in the corner," said John pointing to the big blue steamer trunk in the back right corner of the garage.

Luke looked at the man, "Do you like it here?"

"Yes," said John, "our kids love the area and they go to school at the end of the block."

"So you would like to stay here!" said Luke.

"Yes," said John with a little excitement in his voice.

"Would you like to buy the house?" asked Luke.

"Oh, we couldn't afford to buy," said John. "Our income is just enough to keep us comfortable."

"What are you paying for rent?" asked Luke.

"$1249.00 per month," said John.

"The lawyer keeps $200.00 of that for maintenance and management of the property," said Luke.

"You have been in the house for almost 2 years," stated Luke.

"That's right," said John.

"That comes to a rounded figure of $24,000.00 that you have paid in rent, "said Luke. "Now if I take that as a down payment and carry a mortgage of $1049.00 per month for a period of 40 years, do you think you would be able to afford to own the house?

John stood in the garage looking at Luke with his mouth open, "Um, um, yes," said John.

"Good I'll have my lawyer draw it up and the house is yours," said Luke. "Now give me a hand with this trunk."

Luke backed the truck up to the garage, loaded the trunk and drove away, never to return to that street or area again.

Luke stayed a few weeks in a motel, the big blue steamer trunk sitting in a corner of the room. One day after coming home from work he walked over to the trunk and opened it, the smell of his parents and of his childhood came wafting out hitting him like hot dry air on a July afternoon.

Luke peered inside the open trunk and closed it again. He sat on the bed, tears in his eyes. He got up and locked the trunk, taping the key to the lid. He loaded the trunk in his rented truck and drove to a storage yard, rented a 4 x 8 storage locker and put the trunk in it.

Luke rented an apartment close to his work. Nancy was living on campus during her final year of nursing school, and she would stay with him on her days off from clinics.

During one of these stay overs Luke asked Nancy to marry him.

The answer was an astounding YES.

Luke continued to improve his computer skills and after 6 months on the job he was promoted to assistant head programmer.

Nancy graduated in July, a year after Luke's release from prison.

The following month Nancy and Luke got married.

Nancy was hired by the local hospital, the one where she met Luke for the first time.

Luke and Nancy bought a house and settle in to start a family.

Nancy's nursing job required that she did shift work. Luke found this most difficult when she was on the afternoon shift.

He was always interested in theatre performances and sought out a local theatre group. It was volunteer work but he enjoyed it. He learned the art of makeup, stage lighting and even set up a small computer program for some of the lighting sequences of some of the plays.

On her days off or when she was on the day shift, Nancy would go to the rehearsals with Luke and also do a bit of acting.

About a year later Nancy was pregnant and in due time gave birth to a daughter, Claire.

Luke was very happy in his life and was an excellent husband and father. They would take Claire to the rehearsals with them and to all events that they were invited to.

A few weeks after Claire's 1st birthday, Nancy was again pregnant.

On their way home from the doctor's office, where she had an ultra sound examination revealing she was going to have a boy, a drunk driver ran a red light at a busy intersection. He was driving a ¾ ton pickup truck. The truck slammed into the passenger side of Luke's mini-van, pushing the van into another vehicle.

The passenger side of Luke's van was pushed in so far that the seats on that side of the van were ripped from their bases.

The driver's side was also pushed out from the impact with the other vehicle.

The deployed air bags made it impossible for Luke to see his wife and daughter, who were pinned against the metal from the side of the van.

After the sound of crunching metal and screaming had stopped, there were no sounds at all. Not screaming, not crying, nothing but death. Luke managed to look over toward his wife and then passed out. He didn't see, from the angle that he was looking, the piece of steel sticking into Nancy's temple. Claire was thrown around so violently in her car seat that her little head was bounced from one side of the padding to the other. By the time the collision stopped, Claire's head was bent forward, her chin resting on her chest, delicate little bones sticking out of the back of her neck.

Luke woke up in the hospital, legs broken, his left arm broken and bruises and multiple cuts on his face and upper body.

By his right hand was the call button for the nurse. He pressed it and a nurse came immediately.

"Nancy," said Luke when the nurse entered the room.

The nurse walked up to Luke and he saw that it wasn't Nancy but a friend of theirs that he knew well.

"Judy," said Luke, "how is Nancy and Claire?"

Judy looked at him, tears filling her eyes. "They didn't survive the accident."

Luke broke into tears and put his right arm around Judy as she bent over him to console him.

Luke laid in the bed not saying anything. His world had just been shattered and every sense of feeling in his body was sucked out of him.

Luke was in the hospital for 2 months while his bones healed. In all that time he didn't talk to anyone about the accident that killed his wife and daughter.

The driver of the truck was Lloyd Erickson. He was sentenced to 2 years jail time and a life ban on driving.

Lloyd was assigned to Slade, to be orientated in prison life and kept safe.

As soon as Slade found out that Lloyd was the drunk driver that had killed Luke's family, he put a plan together to have Lloyd killed.

A couple weeks after Lloyd had been in prison, Slade picked a fight with one of the other inmates, Bruce. Slade didn't hurt

Bruce to badly, just enough to warrant disciplinary action. Bruce was sent to the hospital for treatment and Slade was sent to solitary confinement.

Lloyd didn't last 1 month in prison. He was found dead in his cell hanging against the bars of his cell door with his sheet tied around his neck. An apparent suicide. That was the official ruling.

Slade slept very well that night in solitude.

A Different Life

When Luke was released from the hospital he resumed his job. The company had replaced him as assistant to the head programmer and held a position as information coordinator with the company. The new position was to do security checks on potential employees for client companies. It wasn't a high skilled position but it gave him something to work at while he recovered from the loss of his family.

He rented out the house that he and Nancy had bought, not wanting to sell it, at the same time not wanting to live in it. He rented an apartment close to his work.

Luke put all of Nancy's and Claire's stuff in the trunk along with his parent's memorabilia.

Luke no longer had a car or wanting a car. One day as he walked home from work, he saw a driver swerving erratically down the road and almost jumped the curb and hit a child on his bike.

Luke wrote down the license plate number and rushed up to the boy and asked if he was alright. Other than being a little frightened he was fine.

"I saw the man in the car," the boy said, "his eyes were closed when I first saw him then they opened and that's when he turned the car away from me. His face was red and he looked like my daddy does when he gets up in the morning. All groggy eyed."

Luke walked with the boy until they came to the boy's house. "Take care," said Luke as the boy pushed his bike to the side of the house and disappeared behind a gate.

The next day Luke entered the license plate number into his search engine. The one he uses for his work doing security checks.

He got the name and address of the driver and decided to do a little detective work.

After work, Luke went to the neighbourhood where the man lived. There was no car in the driveway so he sat at the bus stop across the street and waited. About 10 minutes later he saw a car speeding up the road and pulling into the driveway of the house he was watching. A man got out and swayed up to the front door and went in. Luke knew from the man's walk that he was drunk.

The next day Luke booked off sick from work and went back to the man's house. He walked up to the door and knocked loudly…. No answer…. He walked around to the back of the house. The back yard needed mowing and there were several children's toys lying in the grass which was growing around and through them.

Luke went to the back door and to his surprise it was unlocked. He went in and looked around. He saw a stack of letters on the corner of the kitchen table and glanced through them. One letter stuck out from the others. .. Divorce papers …..

Luke put the letters back the way he found them and searched the rest of the house. Not much in the house was out of the ordinary, living room furniture, beds and dressers in the bedrooms. He opened a closet door and the inside was full of empty liquor bottles.

It was apparent that he had been drinking for a very long time.

Luke went into the living room and opened the cabinet that was against one wall. In one compartment were several bottles of liquor all unopened. He counted them and made a mental note to the quantity and type.

Luke checked to make sure everything was where is should be and left.

The next day Luke once again phoned in sick and went to the man's house and entered through the unlocked back door. He went to the liquor cabinet in the living room and instantly noticed that one bottle was missing.

Luke thought to himself, "he drinks a bottle in the evening and then drinks after work, or during work, and drives home where he drinks another bottle. I don't think this guy is sober at any time during the day."

Luke went to the local hardware store and purchased some mineral spirits then to the liquor store and bought a bottle of liquor that was the same as what he saw in the man's house.

He went home and carefully removed the bottle cap, not tearing the seal, from the liquor bottle and poured half of the contents out. Then he filled the bottle with the mineral spirits and replaced the cap with the seal.

Luke went back to the man's house and replaced one of the bottles with his own, making sure he wiped the replaced bottle to eliminate his finger prints, and left.

Luke went to work the next day and the next, each day checking the paper for any news of a mysterious death.

On the weekend Luke was watching the news on TV and they mentioned that a Mr. Arnold Wolken was found dead in his home by his estranged wife. It was determined that he died of alcohol poisoning.

Luke sat back in his chair and felt a sense of satisfaction, not from the death of another person but from knowing that someone's child or loved one will not be killed by this person.

A few days later Luke decided to take a walk after dinner. His apartment wasn't far from the neighbourhood pub.

He sat at the bar and ordered a beer. While sipping on his beer he surveyed the patrons of the establishment. He noticed in the back of the pub was a group of young women enjoying a few drinks after work.

He watched them for some time and noticed that one woman was drinking more than the others.

A couple hours later the women got up and left. Luke left shortly after, but kept his attention on the one woman that had been drinking heavily.

After the women said their good byes, three of the women got into a taxi and left. The fourth woman walked to her car and got in. She started the car, put it in reverse and as she backed out of the parking spot lightly nudged the car that was beside her.

Without checking if there was any damage she drove out of the parking lot and raced down the street.

Luke wrote down her license number and walked home.

The next night Luke went to the same pub and sat at the bar. In the back of the room was the same woman, this time having a few drinks with a man. Later they left and Luke followed.

In the parking lot the woman kissed the man bye and he walked to the nearby bus stop. She got in her car and drove off.

The next day at work Luke did a search of her license plate number.

Marie Loupe, age 23, executive secretary.

Luke took down the information as well as the address and phone number. One more search and he had her email address as well.

It was the weekend and Luke sat at the bus stop outside the pub and waited.

Around midnight Marie left the pub and got into her car. One of her friends ran up to the car and tried to get her to take a taxi home. Marie said she was fine and it was just a short distance to her place, and drove off.

Luke went home and turned on his computer. He entered Marie's email address and wrote, "I'm watching you. Don't drink and drive or something terrible will happen."

Using his knowledge of the internet he sent the email via Praque, Indonesia and Thailand.

When Marie opened her email she saw the message. She looked at the sender and noticed it was from outside the country. She deleted the message and considered it a prank or spam and thought nothing of it.

On Monday Luke called in sick at his job and went over to Marie's place.

It was a first floor suite in one of the new buildings several blocks from the pub. Luke walked around the building and didn't see any safe way to get into Marie's suite.

Luke went back home and on his computer accessed the computer used by the concierge and security for the building.

From the files he found the access code to Marie's suite and encoded a key card.

Luke went back to Marie's building and using his key pass opened the main lobby door and then walked down the hall to Marie's suite, opened the door and walked in.

From his searching he knew that Marie lived alone and he would not be bothered by anyone.

Inside, Luke looked around. It was a small apartment, neatly kept. Kitchen, living / dining room, bathroom and bedroom.

In the living room was a large aquarium. Luke walked over to it. No water, but a rather large snake was curled up under a heat lamp.

"Why would anyone want to have a King Cobra as a pet," he said to himself.

Luke bent over and unplugged the heat lamp removed the bulb and shook it several times then replaced the bulb and plugged it back into the wall socket. The heat lamp turned on and immediately went very bright then went out. Luke then slid the cover of the aquarium back a bit so that there was enough space between the lid and top of the aquarium for the snake to get out, if it wanted to.

Luke made sure he left no fingerprints, wiping down the door knob as he left.

That evening Marie arrived home around 8 p.m. She stumbled into the living room and plopped herself on the couch, laying with her head on the arm rest.

From under the cushion of the couch the Cobra struck out at what had disturbed it and bit Marie in the arm.

Marie was half asleep when she plopped down on the couch and didn't react to the bite of the Cobra.

She never woke up.

The next day her work sent someone over to the apartment to find out why she wasn't at work and why she didn't answer her phone when they called.

The concierge opened the door to Marie's suite and they walked into the apartment. There was a faint pungent odour in the air and then they saw Marie laying on the couch. Her body was swollen and her skin was a dark brown color. The Concierge looked over to the aquarium and saw immediately that the lid was askew and the tank was empty.

"We have to leave now," said the concierge to the woman sent from the company. The Concierge knew that Marie kept a cobra.

On the news that evening the top story was about the search for a cobra in a woman's apartment and how the woman was killed by it.

Luke went for a walk that night and enjoyed the quietness of the evening.

A few days later Luke was told that a client wanted to meet with them for an upgrade to their screening process. The

Client was in Miami, Florida and they were to leave the next day.

In Miami Luke and his boss met with the client on the first day over lunch. The CEO of the client company enjoyed several cocktails with lunch. After Lunch another meeting was scheduled at the CEO's home outside of Miami on Miami Beach. The CEO then got in his S-Class Mercedes and drove away.

Luke new that the CEO was over the legal limit for alcohol consumption. That evening Luke sent the CEO an email. "I'm watching you. Don't drink and drive."

The next morning when the CEO opened his email he saw the email and deleted it without looking at it.

Later that morning Luke and his boss drove to Miami Beach using Hwy 195, a beautiful expressway leading from the airport straight to Miami Beach. It only took a few minutes at highway speeds of 70 miles per hour to get to the address given to them.

When they arrived, the CEO showed them around his property and his beach front dock. During the tour Luke managed to get a look at the Mercedes parked in the garage and took note of the Vehicle Identity Number on the dash board.

The CEO put on a fabulous lunch along with lots of drinks.

After Lunch Luke drove the rented car with his boss back to the client company to finalize the contract.

The CEO took his Mercedes.

Luke could plainly see that the CEO was not completely in control of the car and had difficulty keeping up with him. His rate of speed was well over the posted speed limit.

With the contract signed, Luke and his boss went back to the hotel and made arrangements to leave on the next flight out in the morning.

On the flight, Luke was on his computer. He accessed the Mercedes website and read up on all the features of the S-Class Mercedes. Some of the notable features were: Driving Assistance, Steering Assistance, Power Windows, Brake Assist, Electronic Stability Program and Collision Prevention Assist.

At home Luke hacked into the CEO's computer and found the remote access login to the Mercedes diagnostics and accessed the onboard computer.

With a few code adjustments Luke was able to put in a subroutine that would cause the computer to disable all the safety features after the car reached a speed of 70 miles per hour. Luke also coded the accelerator to lock at full speed. With the computer executing the new program the car would race down the interstate, a collision was imminent.

The next morning Luke listened to the news while he ate his breakfast. On the news was mentioned that a Mr. Paul Chevo lost control of his Mercedes and crashed through the guard railing on the interstate 195 and plunged into the water of Biscayne Bay, Florida.

Luke went to work and talked to his boss about the terrible accident of Paul Chevo, CEO of the company they had just been with in Miami.

Luke had mentally adjusted to his own accident and thought it time to buy a condo. A co-worker had recently bought a home and he asked if he could recommend a good REALTOR. He gave Luke his Realtor's business card.

Luke phoned Mr. Roland Vork, the real estate agent that was recommended to him. He told Roland that he was interested in buying a condo close to his work. Roland said that there were plenty of nice condos in the area and that he would arrange a view later that day.

Roland was waiting in the lobby of the first building he wanted to show, when Luke arrived. They greeted and Luke caught the faint odour of alcohol on Roland's breath. They went into the elevator and the smell of alcohol and tobacco on his breath was even stronger.

On the 9th floor Roland walked out of the elevator and up to unit 903, unlocked the door and walked in.

Luke followed Roland in and looked around the vacant apartment. "Nice," he said, and walked around checking out the different rooms. "What else do you have, I would like to see a couple others."

"Of course," said Roland. "Here is a feature sheet of another condo just around the corner. I can set up an appointment for tomorrow evening."

Luke took the feature sheet and said, "That's great."

Luke watched as Roland got in his car and drove away, noting the license plate number. He went inside the condo tower and sat in the lobby and sent Roland an email, "I'm watching you. Don't drink and drive."

Luke studied the feature sheet that Roland gave him. This condo was also vacant. He accessed the condo website and then was able to access the concierge computer and got the access code to the unit that he was going to be shown the next day.

Luke walked over to the new condo tower and entered. At the elevator he entered the code for the floor he wanted and on that floor went to the unit and entered the entry code.

Inside Luke checked out the balcony and the kitchen. The kitchen had a gas stove. He walked over to the balcony again and jabbed the folded up feature sheet into the track of the door so it wouldn't open. Then he went to the breaker box and turned off the power to the air conditioning unit.

He knew that Roland would check out the unit before he showed it to Luke.

Luke calculated that if he turned the burners on the stove and blew out the flames that it would take about 6 hours to create a combustible atmosphere in the unit.

Most buildings are smoke free and this one was no exception. Roland was a heavy smoker and he hoped that he would have a lit cigarette in his hand or mouth when he entered the unit.

Luke sent Roland one more email, "I'm watching you …… Don't drink and drive."

The next morning Roland called Luke to verify the viewing that evening and also said he got the weirdest email.

"Oh," said Luke.

"Yes. It said 'I'm watching you. Don't drink and drive.'" Said Roland.

"That is weird," said Luke. "What are you going to do about it?"

"I have already deleted it. Doesn't make any sense."

"Do you drink and drive?" asked Luke.

"Sometimes, but I have it under control," said Roland.

"Don't get caught," said Luke.

"Have a good day Luke," said Roland as he shrugged off the suggestion and hung up the phone.

Luke went back to work on his computer. He did a search of Mr. Roland Vork. …. I charge of impaired driving 5 years ago. …. "Hm, back on the sauce, are you," he thought to himself.

At lunch Luke went back to the condo and went into the unit and turned all the burners on the stove to the 'high' position and extinguished the flames.

At home Luke sent Roland a text message. "Something has come up, I can't make the appointment." He sent the message to Roland only a few minutes before the meet.

After texting Roland, Luke went to the pub and met a few friends from the office. "Glad to see that you could make it," they said as he sat down.

Roland was already in the elevator and decided to check out the unit anyway. Being frustrated over the cancelled appointment he lit a cigarette once out of the elevator. He walked over to the unit and unlocked the door and walked in. He hadn't gotten two steps inside when the fumes in the condo ignited from his cigarette. The explosion was so severe that the balcony door was blown out tumbling to the courtyard below. Roland was blown backwards into the hallway, his entire front, was instantly charred. The hot air from the explosion incinerated his lungs. The heat was so intense that when he was slammed into the wall of the corridor his suite fused with the corridor wall permanently securing him against it.

The fire department was immediately called when the explosion was heard by the concierge. The police were also called when the firemen discovered Roland fused with the corridor wall.

At the pub Luke smiled and thanked them for the invite. While he was enjoying the company of his friends he noticed a woman about his age sitting by herself drinking.

She was a beautiful looking woman in her early twenties, black hair flowing across her shoulders.

Luke asked his friends if they knew her, since they came to the same pub quite often.

"We've seen her before," they said. "Usually with a guy."

His friends looked at Luke and smiled, "Go ahead go talk to her."

Luke got up and walked over where she was sitting. "Hi I'm Luke. Would you like to join my friends and me," gesturing to the table he just come from.

"I don't know," she said.

Luke smiled at her, "Please," he said and held out his hand.

"OK," she said shyly. "I'm Amie"

Amie was about 5 foot 8 inches tall with a slim figure.

Luke was immediately attracted to her.

They had a great time and when it was time to leave Amie took her car keys out of her purse.

Luke looked at her, "you aren't going to drive your car are you?"

Amie looked at the keys then at Luke. "Maybe I shouldn't," and gave them to Luke.

"Do you live far from here, "asked Luke?

"A couple blocks," she said. "I stopped here after work."

"I'll walk you home."

As they walked Amie told Luke that she just recently broke up with her boyfriend of 3 years, and she was sad and upset about the breakup.

"Lucky day for me," said Luke reaching out and taking her hand in his.

"Maybe for both of us," said Amie, blushing.

The next morning Luke went to the pub and got Amie's car and drove it to her apartment building. He went up to her apartment and knocked on the door.

Amie opened the door, "What are you doing here?" she asked.

"Returning your car keys," said Luke handing her the keys. "The car is parked down stairs in front of the building."

"Thank you," said Aimie turning to close the door.

Luke looked at her and noticed she had fresh make applied heavily to her left cheek. "You OK?" he asked.

"Yes I'm fine," she said keeping her face turned away from him.

"You're not fine," said Luke, placing his hand gently on her shoulder.

Immediately Amie turned and hugged Luke. "I'm afraid," she said. "Jerry was here last night when I got home. He was drunk and I told him to leave. He grabbed me and when I tried to fight him off he hit me across the cheek." She hugged Luke harder and began to cry.

Luke hugged her back and told her that he wouldn't let anything more happen to her, and with him she could feel safe.

She looked up at him and pulled him down a little and kissed him. "Thank You."

Luke stayed with Amie for the rest of the morning. They talked and had breakfast together. Luke was sitting at the breakfast table and watched Amie as she cooked some bacon and eggs. He noticed how her shoulder length hair flowed as she hurried with the breakfast. How she moved from the kitchen counter to the table.

"What are you looking at?" said asked.

"You," said Luke with a smile on his face.

After breakfast they sat in the living room and talked about their lives. When Amie went into the kitchen to clear the table and do the dishes Luke took the opportunity to look around. He found some mail on a side table. One of the letters was addressed to Jerry Smithers. Luke made a mental note of the name.

When Amie came back Luke told her that he had some work to do and asked her out for dinner that evening.

"I'll pick you up at 7," said Luke.

"OK," said Amie as she kissed him bye and closed the door.

Luke was on Roland's appointment list at the real estate office and the police contacted him asking him to come down to the police station.

They asked him where he was that evening.

Luke explained to them that he had a rough day and didn't feel like viewing the condo and sent Roland a text to that fact. He said he went to the pub and had some drinks with friends.

Everything checked out and the official report stated it as an accident, an unfortunate accident.

The police contacted Luke after the investigation and said that he was lucky that he hadn't kept the appointment as there was a faulty gas valve on the stove.

Luke picked up Amie at 7. He noticed a '76 Camaro parked about half a block away with a man sitting inside.

Luke and Amie walked out of her apartment building, her arm clenching his as they walked.

"Your car," said Luke. "Do you want me to drive or you?"

Amie looked at Luke a smile on her face and handed him the keys.

Luke opened the passenger door for her then went to the driver's side. Before he got into the car he looked once more at the Camaro and took note of the license plate number.

Luke and Amie had an enjoyable dinner with laughter and flirts.

When Luke finally brought Amie back to her place he checked to see if the Camaro was still parked on the street. It was and the man inside was drinking something from a bottle.

Standing at the entrance to the apartment building Luke said, "Amie I don't want you to spend the night alone. Not until we are sure Jerry isn't going to come around and hurt you."

Amie looked at Luke tenderly, "I don't think he will bother me."

"Never the less, I don't want you alone tonight. I'll sleep on the couch."

"If you insist, but the couch isn't very big or comfortable," said Amie.

"It will be fine," smiled Luke.

When Jerry saw that Luke went inside with Amie he was furious. He sat in his car for another twenty minutes and when Luke didn't come out he finished the last of the bottle of Southern Comfort and tossed it out the window smashing against a building wall. Then he started the car and recklessly drove off down the street.

The next morning, Sunday, Luke and Amie decided to explore the country side. They packed a picnic lunch and headed towards the Lake District. They spent the entire day together. On the way home Luke stopped and picked up a new lock for Amie's apartment door.

He installed the new lock and made sure it was secure.

"Work tomorrow early," said Luke. "I'll call you in the morning."

Amie kissed him long and hard. "Thank you."

On his way out of the building Luke checked the road to see if he saw the Camaro parked. It wasn't there and as he walked to his own apartment he took notice of the alley ways to make sure Jerry wasn't hiding down one of them.

At work Luke did a search on Jerry Smithers and the Camaro.

Jerry Smithers was charged with aggravated assault twice, and one weapons charge.

Luke got the home address for Jerry and during lunch went to that address.

Jerry seemed to be away so he let himself into the run down low-rise apartment building.

A quick search Luke found a hand gun and ammunition. He took the gun and left the building.

He called Amie when he returned to work after lunch and said that he had to work late and he would call her later that evening.

Luke left work about 4 and went home where he put on some of the theatrical disguises that he still had in a suite case. He then went to Jerry's apartment. When he arrived Jerry was just getting home. A few minutes later Jerry came back out and got in his car and drove off.

Luke hailed a taxi and followed Jerry to a pub a few blocks away.

Luke went into the pub and sat at the bar and ordered a beer.

Jerry was sitting at a table and from the time Luke had walked into the bar, Jerry had already belted down two drinks and was pouring another large glass of Southern Comfort.

Luke got up from the bar and staggered pass Jerry accidently bumping into him, putting a sleeping potion into Jerry's glass.

Luke continued to stagger out to the parking lot.

About a half hour later Jerry, barely able to walk, managed to get to his car and get into the driver's side. Before he could close the door, Luke rushed over and pushed Jerry over to the passenger side, flipping him over the stick shift consol. Jerry sat in the passenger seat eyes half shut staring at Luke.

Luke drove the car to a secluded spot in the industrial area of the city.

By this time Jerry was passed out.

Luke stopped the car and placed Jerry in the driver's seat. He took the gun out of his pocket and checked that the gun had one bullet in the chamber. He put the gun in Jerry's right hand and put a few drops of crazy glue on the handle so that it would bond to his hand.

Luke started the car and put Jerry's foot on the gas pedal just enough so that the car would start moving. He put the car in gear and stepped away. The car started moving slowly at first but quickly picked up speed. The car headed straight toward a large cement highway divider. The car was going about 15 mph when it impacted the barrier.

Luke had purchased a disposable cell phone and now called 911. "I just saw a car ram into a concrete barrier on Terminal Avenue in the industrial section. It looks like the driver has a gun." Luke hung up and walked away.

Several minutes later a police car, ambulance, and fire truck arrived on the scene.

By this time Jerry had woken up and was trying to get out of the car.

A policeman approached the car, but stopped short when he saw the gun in Jerry's hand.

"Drop the gun," yelled the policeman.

Jerry was confused and disoriented. He hadn't notice the gun in his hand. He stumbled a couple steps from the car in the direction of the policeman.

"Drop the gun," repeated the policeman.

By this time a second police car arrived and two more policemen got out.

Jerry still confused kept walking towards the policemen. At one point he stumbled and the gun discharged and the bullet shot into the ground several feet in front of him.

Immediately the three policemen opened fire and shot Jerry several times.

Jerry fell backwards, arms flaring out from his body. As his lifeless body hit the ground his arms struck the concrete surface of the road a second later then bounced up and fell back. The gun that was in his hand was dislodged and fell to the ground.

The ambulance attendants went over to Jerry after the policemen motioned that it was safe. They checked for a pulse, but found none. They picked him up and placed him in a black body bag, zipped it and placed him on the gurney and wheeled him over to the ambulance, and headed for the morgue.

Luke was at Amie's place when the police went there the following evening.

They told her that Jerry was killed during an altercation with the police the night before. He was drunk and wielding a gun.

Amie started to cry and said she wasn't surprised that something like that happened. She told the police that the reason she broke up with him was because of his drinking and wild nature.

Luke comforted her, holding her in his arms. "I'm sorry," he said softly.

Amie was too upset to go for dinner and told Luke that she would like to be alone.

Luke asked her out for dinner the following night, which she agreed to.

At dinner Amie told Luke that she was an executive secretary to a stock broker CEO and that she had met Jerry at one of the stock broker events. She knew that Jerry was a heavy drinker and she also started drinking heavily when she was dating him.

"A few months ago I woke up in Jerry's apartment and I don't remember how I got there," she said. "I never stayed at his apartment, he always came to mine."

"After that I stopped drinking which put a split between us. Jerry liked to party and drinking was always involved. Eventually I told him that this wasn't working out and I didn't want to be associated with him as long as he drank."

"When we met at the bar, that was the first drink I had since I stopped months ago," she said. "Jerry didn't think I was serious about leaving him. That's why he came over to the apartment the other night. He had been drinking of course, and said he didn't want to lose me. When I told him it was over he called me a bitch and hit me and left. I didn't think he would be back and I definitely didn't think he would do anything as stupid as taking his gun with him to a bar."

"I'm looking at buying a condo. I'm viewing some tomorrow. Would you like to come along?" asked Luke changing the subject, seeing that Amie was getting upset.

"That sounds interesting," said Amie. "But I have some organizing to do. Jerry left lots of stuff at my place and I want to clean it out. Take it to Big Brothers."

"Need any help?" offered Luke.

"No I'm fine with doing it by myself," she said.

Luke took Amie home and said good night at the main entrance to her apartment and went home.

The next day Luke viewed a few condo units and decided on one that was very close to his work. It was ideal for him. It had two bedrooms, one which he was going to use as an office.

After signing the papers he went for a walk around his new neighbourhood. As he turned a corner he saw a blue Mazda slowly swerving along the road. He immediately took down the license number.

When he got home he turned on his computer and accessed the motor vehicle office, which he was allowed to for his business, and put in the license number.

He was shocked when he saw the name come up on the monitor.

Amie Johnson was the name showing as the registered owner of the car and gave the address, the same as his Amie.

Luke logged out and turned the computer off.

Later that night he sent Amie an email. "I'm watching you. Don't drink and drive."

He sent it as usual so that the origin could not be traced.

For the next couple days Luke tried to get in touch with Amie, but every time she was either not home or unavailable to meet with him.

About a week after Luke saw her driving her car he got an email from Amie. "Luke I'm not ready for a serious commitment right now. You seem to be a really great guy, but I have issues that I have to deal with before I can get involved with someone..... bye.... Amie."

Luke was hurt that she would tell him like this, but not all together surprised. He had thought something was going on in her life that he didn't know about. After thinking about it for a few minutes he came to the conclusion that this was the best way.

That evening he was at his new place cleaning and moving in a few boxes and getting ready for the movers to bring in the rest of his furniture the next day. On his way back to his rental he saw Amie in her Blue Mazda driving down the street in a chaotic manner.

He grabbed his cell phone and called 911 and told them about a drunk driver going down 5th Street. He didn't give them his name and he used the disposable phone that he had bought earlier.

When he got home he sent Amie another email, "I'm watching you, don't drink and drive."

The next day was a busy day with the movers loading his furniture from the rental and moving it to his new condo. It was late in the afternoon when everything was unloaded and in their proper place.

Luke went to the neighbourhood restaurant for dinner. At the restaurant he saw Amie with a man. They were sitting on the other side of the restaurant and Amie's back was towards him.

He sat down and ordered his food. He watched Amie and her friend and noticed that there was a large amount of wine being consumed.

Luke finished his meal and left. He stood outside the restaurant in a covered doorway and waited for Amie and her friend to come out.

Luke saw Amie's car parked in the Restaurant's parking lot. Eventually she came out of the restaurant and said good bye to the man and walked over to her car. She took the keys out of her purse and looked at them for a second or two. Then gave a little shrug and opened the car door, got in and drove away.

Luke didn't bother calling 911 a second time. Nothing was done the first time he called.

Luke sent Amie one last email. "I'm watching you. Don't drink and Drive. This is your last warning."

Over the next few days Luke saw Amie and the blue Mazda a couple times swerving down the road.

Luke knew this had to stop. He did more investigation into Amie's life. He also checked into her position at the brokerage firm.

He discovered that at the end of every month Amie would deliver some stock forms to a client in the country.

At the end of the month Luke rented a car and followed Amie to the client's house.

She delivered the papers and stayed for lunch. When she came out of the house Luke was watching from a secluded spot on the hill side. He could see that she had been drinking.

Luke got in his car and drove back towards town. As he approached a steep turn he had an idea. The visibility on this section of highway was very limited. As the road descended it also turned sharply, you couldn't see more than a few feet in front of you.

Luke turned off on a 'run-away lane'

He got out and picked up a few large rocks that where lying on the side of the road. He then put them on the road so that whoever came along they would either hit the rocks or swerve to miss them. The speed limit along this section was slow enough that a car coming around the curve would have plenty of time to stop.

Luke went back to his car and waited. Soon Amie came around the bend in the road, travelling faster then she should have. By the time she saw the rocks in the road, it was too late. She slammed on her brakes and the car immediately turned to the right and hit the rocks on the driver's side of the car. The car continued to head for the bank where there was a 100 foot drop off. The car smashed through the safety rail and plunged down the ravine.

Luke got in his car and drove away.

A few minutes later another car came along, saw the rocks in the road and saw the safety rail broken. The driver stopped the car and looked over the cliff to the ravine below. At the bottom was the blue Mazda. The police were called along with the fire rescue team.

Once they got down the steep cliff face they checked the car and found Amie in the front seat. She was dead. She didn't have her seat belt on and when the car hit the bottom of the ravine she flew forward her chest crunching against the steering wheel and her head hitting the windshield.

The Police determined that the cause of the accident was a combination of alcohol and excessive speed.

Luke was turning more and more into a recluse. He would go to work and from there straight home. The death of Amie was weighing on his mind. He did what he had to do to stop her from hurting or killing someone. What he didn't understand was why people didn't use common sense when they drank alcohol. During the time he spent in his condo he slowly came to the realization that alcohol destroys the ability to think straight.

He resolved that he would have to do more to get the message out that drinking and driving was dangerous. From that day on he decided to go to the pub after work and find the people that drank excessively and then drive their car.

On one of these evenings Luke was working on his second beer. He noticed a man at one of the tables becoming louder and louder as he spoke. He was with another man and a woman. He paid special attention on the one person who was getting quite drunk. A couple hours passed and the man ordered a coffee and went to the men's room. When he came back he drank the coffee hastily and said good bye to the man and woman and left.

Luke followed him out and saw the man walk over to his car and get in. He noticed that the man put something in his mouth before he started the car. The man sat up very straight in the driver's seat and slowly manoeuvred the car out of the parking lot and drove down the street .... slowly.

Luke wrote down the license number and walked the short distance home.

At home he turned on his computer and entered the license number into his search program. After a few seconds the name Harold Basks came up. Luke read the report .... no driving violations and no criminal record. He worked as a reporter at the local newspaper. The information also showed his email address.

THE INTERNET KILLER

Luke did an internet search and found out that his wife of 15 years had recently passed away and he was alone, not having any children.

Luke sent Harold an email: "Don't drink and drive. I'm watching you".

The next morning when Harold got to his office, he grabbed a cup of coffee and went to his desk. As usual the first thing he did after turning the computer on was to check his email.

There it was "Don't drink and drive. I'm watching you". In large type letters.

Harold tried to find who sent the email but the technician at the news paper said it was impossible to trace. The technician also said it was probably local.

Harold went back to his desk and sat thinking about the message in the email. He put a note on his calendar and filed the email in his "Unusual" mail box.

A couple days later Luke saw Harold again at the pub. This time he was with two men and they were having a loud conversation. Luke watched as they left and the three of them got into Harold's car and slowly drove off.

Luke sent Harold another email: "Don't drink and drive. I'm watching you."

At his office Harold saw the message when he opened his email. "Who is this guy," he thought to himself. He decided to do a short story about the email and see what happens.

It was a filler piece somewhere in the middle of the paper. It read:

"A friend of mine received an email the other day. The email had this in large print; "Don't drink and drive. I'm watching you." It sounds like some disturbed person is playing with people's minds. If you have received a similar email, I would like to know.... Harold Basks"

Someone at Luke's work saw the article and brought it to work and was showing everyone in the office. Luke looked at the article and smiled. "Weird isn't it," he said to the person with the article, and went back to work.

About a week later Luke saw Harold at the same pub. Harold as usual was drinking heavily and afterwards drove home.

Luke booked off sick the next day and went to Harold's house. The house was in a nice neighbourhood on a quiet cul-de-sac. He went up to the door and knocked. As he waited for someone to open the door he looked around to see if anyone was watching. Of course no one answered his knocking and sure that no one was watching he walked around to the back yard where he saw a large propane tank used to fuel the house. On inspecting the tank he saw a shut off valve installed at the base of the tank, tucked underneath. It would be hard to reach, but if a person lay on the ground they could work their way over to the valve.

Luke left the yard and went to Work World to buy a pair of coveralls. Harold's house backed onto a green belt with trails. Harold's back yard had a fence dividing his yard from the right away. The fence was a steel post and wire and only 4 feet tall, easy to get over.

That evening when he saw that Harold was home, he jumped the fence and lay on the cement pad that supported the propane tank, he worked his way under the tank and with his outstretching arm he could just reach the shut off valve. The valve was old and Luke had to twist hard on the handle to get the valve moving. He managed to turn the valve off. He waited about 30 seconds and turned the valve back on.

Making sure that he didn't leave any evidence behind Luke jumped the fence and walked down the path to his rented car.

It was three days before anyone decided to check on Harold. Even though he didn't show up for work the next day, everyone thought he might be following a story.

A neighbour was the one who called the police, because the papers and mail was piling up on the porch. "Harold never left the papers or mail on the porch," said the neighbour to the police.

The policeman knocked on the door, but there was no answer. He walked around to the back yard and checked the back door. It was locked. When he noticed the propane tank, he immediately thought of a propane leak in the house and called the fire department to come and check the house for propane.

A detection unit was dispatched to the house and a probe was inserted into the house through a small hole drilled through the back door of the house. The probe registered a high quantity of propane inside the house.

Propane is an odourless heavy flammable gas. It replaces breathable air in a confined space by pushing it upwards. Propane dissipates quickly in open areas and isn't a problem. The fire department set up large fans at the front door, then opened the front and back doors at the same time and turned on the fan. The fan blew all the propane out of the house and it safely broke down as it dissipated into the outside air.

Inside they found Harold in his bed. The propane replaced the air and he didn't wake up, dyeing in his sleep.

Luke is still out there seeking those who drink and drive. So if you get an email:

Don't drink and drive. I'm watching you.

Take it very seriously. You might not live to regret it.

www.ingramcontent.com/pod-product-compliance
Lightning Source LLC
LaVergne TN
LVHW011726060526
838200LV00051B/3045